"Go Away And Leave Me Alone."

"What if I did?" Rafe crossed the kitchen, stopping when he was directly behind Holly. "Wouldn't you hate it if I left you alone?"

"No. It's what I want," she insisted.

"What about what *I* want?" Her mouth was moist and softly swollen, her eyes glazed and slumberous. Bedroom eyes, he thought. "I want you, Holly. I want to make love to you. I've been waiting for the right time, and that is now. We've spent every day together for nearly a month. You can't say we don't know each other well."

Holly twined her arms around his neck, her fingers combing through his sleek dark hair. She didn't want him to go away and leave her alone—ever....

Dear Reader,

This month, Silhouette Desire celebrates sensuality. All six steamy novels perfectly describe those unique pleasures that gratify our senses, like *seeing* the lean body of a cowboy at work, *smelling* his earthy scent, *tasting* his kiss…and *hearing* him say, "I love you."

Feast your eyes on June's MAN OF THE MONTH, the tall, dark and incredibly handsome single father of four in beloved author Barbara Boswell's *That Marriageable Man!* In bestselling author Lass Small's continuing series, THE KEEPERS OF TEXAS, a feisty lady does her best to tame a reckless cowboy and he winds up unleashing *her* wild side in *The Hard-To-Tame Texan*. And a dating service guarantees delivery of a husband-to-be in *Non-Refundable Groom* by ultrasexy writer Patty Salier.

Plus, Modean Moon unfolds the rags-to-riches story of an honorable lawman who fulfills a sudden socialite's deepest secret desire in *Overnight Heiress*. In Catherine Lanigan's *Montana Bride,* a bachelor hero introduces love and passion to a beautiful virgin. And a rugged cowboy saves a jilted lady in *The Cowboy Who Came in From the Cold* by Pamela Macaluso.

These six passionate stories are sure to leave you tingling… and anticipating next month's sensuous selections. Enjoy!

Regards,

Melissa Senate

Melissa Senate
Senior Editor
Silhouette Books

Please address questions and book requests to:
Silhouette Reader Service
U.S.: 3010 Walden Ave., P.O. Box 1325, Buffalo, NY 14269
Canadian: P.O. Box 609, Fort Erie, Ont. L2A 5X3

BARBARA BOSWELL

THAT MARRIAGEABLE MAN!

SILHOUETTE *Desire*®

Published by Silhouette Books
America's Publisher of Contemporary Romance

SILHOUETTE BOOKS

ISBN 0-373-76147-3

THAT MARRIAGEABLE MAN!

Copyright © 1998 by Barbara Boswell

This edition published by arrangement with Harlequin Books S.A.

® and TM are trademarks of Harlequin Books S.A., used under license.
Trademarks indicated with ® are registered in the United States Patent
and Trademark Office, the Canadian Trade Marks Office and in other
countries.

Printed in U.S.A.

Books by Barbara Boswell

Silhouette Desire

Rule Breaker #558
Another Whirlwind Courtship #583
The Bridal Price #609
The Baby Track #651
License To Love #685
Double Trouble #749
Triple Treat #787
The Best Revenge #821
Family Feud #877
*The Engagement Party #932
The Wilde Bunch #943
Who's the Boss? #1069
The Brennan Baby #1123
That Marriageable Man! #1147

Silhouette Books

Fortune's Children
Stand-In Bride

*Always a Bridesmaid!

BARBARA BOSWELL

loves writing about families. "I guess family has been a big influence on my writing," she says. "I particularly enjoy writing about how my characters' family relationships affect them."

When Barbara isn't writing and reading, she's spending time with her *own* family—her husband, three daughters and three cats, who she concedes are the true bosses of their home! She has lived in Europe, but now makes her home in Pennsylvania. She collects miniatures and holiday ornaments, tries to avoid exercise and has somehow found the time to write over twenty category romances.

One

"Holly, are you sure you want to do it? You really want to go there?" Brenna Worth studied her longtime friend Holly Casale, not bothering to mask her concern. Or her disbelief.

"Not you, too!" Holly shook her head and managed a laugh. A slight one. "I've been defending my decision to the family for weeks, and I hoped I wouldn't have to do it with you, Brenna. Can't you be happy for me? It's a great opportunity. I'll be the only psychiatrist with the Widmark family practice, which is one of the biggest in the city, so I won't have to go begging for referrals like a newcomer normally would. And I've already been asked to serve as a volunteer with the Teens At Risk Task Force and a peer counseling program at one of the high schools."

"All that's in addition to your job? Sounds like they plan to run you ragged with volunteering."

"It's an ideal way for me to get involved with the community and to work with kids. You know that's my main field of interest, Brenna."

"Troubled teens aren't kids, they're hazards—to be avoided," stated Brenna. "I'm so disappointed you aren't moving back here,

Holly. Your mom said you had three good offers all within an hour's drive. It would be great if we lived in the same area again! And to be perfectly honest with you, how happy can I be when your new job is in *South Dakota?*"

"Careful, Brenna, you're starting to sound like my mother. When I told Mom I was moving to Sioux Falls her first words were, 'If you want to move to a place far away with bad weather, why not Alaska? At least there is supposed to be a surplus of eligible men.'"

"And then, inevitably, one of your aunts chimed in with...?" prompted Brenna. She knew Holly's family well.

"Aunt Hedy said, 'With the shortage of marriageable women in Alaska, you're bound to find a man up there, dear,'" Holly quoted with a wry smile.

Brenna sighed. "They just don't give up, do they?"

"No. And they won't until I'm either married or dead. I've already received five copies of *The Rules.* In hardcover." Holly opened her closet door and brought out multiple copies of the book, which offered women advice on how to coyly lure Mr. Right to the altar.

"Mom bought me the book the day it appeared in the stores. Then Aunt Hedy and Aunt Honoria each gave me one. The copies from my cousins Hillary and Heather arrived in the mail on the same day. My sister keeps quizzing me on the contents to see if I've read the book yet. The whole family firmly believes I need all the help I can get when it comes to landing a husband."

"Subtlety has never been your family's strong suit, Holly."

"Not where men and marriage are concerned. Feel free to keep a copy for yourself, Bren." Holly chuckled. "After all, you're still single, too. You might find some useful pointers if you decide you want to acquire a—"

"Don't even joke about it!" Brenna cut in, backing away from the books as if they were radioactive. "I acquire companies, not men. My career keeps me way too busy to even think about the noxious pursuit of husband-hunting."

"My family would consider that blasphemy. Or maybe insanity." Holly's smile faded a little. "You see why I can't come back home to work, don't you, Brenna? I love my family dearly, but my visits here over the years have already given me a taste of what it would be like if I lived among my relatives full-time."

Brenna knew. "An endless succession of setups with any man deemed marriageable by your mother and your sister, and your aunts and cousins."

"And their idea of an eligible bachelor runs a wide gamut, from the twenty-two-year-old video games fanatic to the sixty-one-year-old widower who owns his own real estate agency and has two daughters older than me." Holly heaved a reminiscent groan.

The heart knows no age limit, Aunt Hedy had said blithely. She was the one who'd fixed Holly up with the real estate agent, already a grandfather five times over.

A young man needs the guiding hand of a loving older woman, said Aunt Honoria. The video games nut, a college student who'd looked and acted not a day over sixteen, had been her contribution to the collective Marry-Off-Holly effort.

Your aunts love you, they care about you, they know a woman isn't happy without a husband. Helene Casale, Holly's mother, made no apologies for her two sisters' matchmaking attempts.

No wonder. Mom had been responsible for her own selection of dud blind dates for Holly. The pet shop owner whose sole topics of conversation were tropical fish and reptiles. The lawyer who specialized in personal injury suits and bribed ambulance drivers to beep him so he could arrive at accident scenes to pass out his cards. There had been others, though none quite as memorably horrific.

Holly's older sister Hope and their cousins, Hillary, Heather, and Hayley—all married—had also done their share for "The Cause" over the years, producing a contingent of men whom Holly was lovingly bullied into meeting. Sometimes the men actually were nice, normal and perfectly adequate human beings. Sometimes there would be second dates and even a few more after that.

But so far, friendship rather than romance had resulted in every case because both Holly and the selected matrimonial candidate would recognize that their budding relationship was fated to be platonic, not romantic.

The female members of the clan were in despair that Holly, who had countless male friends, had never come close to nabbing that ultimate prize—an engagement ring. To be followed by the traditional big white wedding. Then the nagging to produce children could rightfully begin. Both Hillary and Heather already had a daughter apiece. Hope and Hayley were each trying zealously to conceive.

"I guess the fact that little Heidi is engaged and planning her wedding hasn't made things any easier for you." Brenna was sympathetic.

Little Heidi was Holly's youngest cousin, who'd turned twenty last month and was currently flashing a minute solitaire on her finger. Though barely a diamond chip bought with the twenty-one-year-old husband-to-be's student loan money, it was still an engagement ring provided by an authentic fiancé.

"Poor Mom. I felt so sorry for her when Heidi announced her engagement at the family's monthly brunch." Holly grimaced at the memory. "Mom claimed she was thrilled about little Heidi's engagement but she left shortly afterward. She claimed she'd been food poisoned, but we all knew why she really felt sick."

"Never mind that she has a daughter who graduated with honors from the University of Michigan's med school and completed a psychiatric residency there." Brenna's blue eyes flashed. "That doesn't count because Honoria is the one meeting with bridal consultants and shopping with Heidi for her wedding gown."

"True. The fact that I'm twenty-nine without a single prospective son-in-law in sight is what really counts as far as Mom is concerned," Holly said dryly.

"God, Holly, it makes me furious on your behalf! Furious and...and crazy."

"Don't be. And as a newly board-certified shrink, I advise you to redirect your anger into something positive. Like making plans to visit me in Sioux Falls as soon as I get settled in. Promise you'll come soon, Bren."

"I promise." Brenna nodded her head. "And it'll have to be soon because doesn't winter come early there? Like around the first of September?"

"South Dakota is not in the Arctic Circle, Brenna. And considering some of the winters we've had here in Michigan, we really have no room to mock the weather anywhere else.''

"You're getting defensive about your new hometown already. I guess you'll fit in out there in Frontier Land. Well, Sioux Falls is lucky to have you, Holly. I just hope that you'll..." Brenna paused, an unholy gleam in her eyes. "That you'll meet the man of your dreams there. Imagine the thrill of being deluged with *Planning the Perfect Wedding Guides* from all your approving relatives!''

There was a knock on the door and Helene Casale entered Holly's bedroom.

"How is the packing coming, Holly?" she asked, glancing at the suitcases that lay opened and half full on the bed.

"It's coming along fairly well, Mom."

"Don't forget to pack this, Holly. You never know when you might need it for reference." Helene Casale put a copy of *The Rules* into the suitcase, then handed one of the books to Brenna. "And you take one, too, dear. The authors practically guarantee a proposal if you follow their advice. Rumor has it that J.F.K. Jr.'s bride was a *Rules* girl."

Holly's eyes met Brenna's and she read her friend's silent message. Accepting the offer to join the Widmark family practice in Sioux Falls, South Dakota, far from her ever-loving, ever-obsessed-with-her-marital-status relatives, was definitely the right move.

The plane touched down at the Sioux Falls airport nearly two hours after its scheduled arrival time, the delay resulting from a mechanical problem discovered in Minneapolis shortly before takeoff.

Rafe Paradise glanced at his watch again.

"Watching the clock isn't going to make the time pass any faster." His seatmate, a petite blonde in a chic gray suit spoke up, her tone amused. "It's ten minutes past the last time you checked. You really are in a hurry to get home, aren't you?"

"Actually, no." Rafe managed to return her smile. There was a difference between *wanting* to get home and *having* to get back as soon as possible, though he didn't feel like discussing the whys and wherefores with the pretty woman sitting next to him.

She'd been flirting with him all during the flight and had already ascertained that he wasn't married, that he was a lawyer who lived in Sioux Falls and had no significant other in his life. Rafe had answered her very direct questions without posing any of his own, but the blonde kept the conversation going, undeterred by his perfunctory responses.

He now knew that her name was Lorna Larson, that she lived and worked in the Twin Cities and was making one of her frequent business trips to Sioux Falls. ("Thanks to the deregulation of telecommunications, Sioux Falls has become a major center of credit card processing and telemarketing," Lorna, a self-proclaimed rising star in a telecommunications company, explained to him.)

As if he, a lifelong native of the city, didn't already know. Still, Rafe made no comment. Why bother to go through the motions—the flirtatious smiles, the eye contact, the exchange of personal info and other requisite preliminaries? As soon as he mentioned his *situation,* the come-hither glow in Lorna Larson's eyes would turn to frost.

Worse, he didn't care. His interest in sex had sunk to ground zero, Rafe acknowledged grimly, because the lack of female companionship in his life no longer even bothered him. Since he'd inherited his two younger half sisters last year—there were other words he could use to describe how they'd happened to land in his life but "inherited" was the most charitable—his social life had become as extinct as the Neanderthals who once inhabited the earth.

Maybe he was on to unlocking the mystery of their disappearance from the planet, Rafe mused darkly. Their caves had been besieged with kids—other people's, not their own—who'd worked them over so thoroughly that their sexual drive had been effectively obliterated. The species had faded from sheer lack of time, interest and energy in sex.

Rafe could definitely relate. He couldn't even remember the last time he'd had sex. Certainly before Camryn and Kaylin had moved in with him. Before his Little Brother Trent and Trent's kid brother Tony had gradually become residents instead of visitors to his house. His last few dates, months and months ago, had ended in disaster because crises with the kids had disrupted them in grand style.

Lorna Larson pressed her business card into Rafe's hand as they reached for their carry-on luggage stored in the overhead compartments. "I wrote the name of the hotel where I'm staying while I'm here in town. Give me a call and we can get together for drinks." Her smile promised much more. She was clearly in the mood for some action during her stay in Sioux Falls.

Rafe murmured a polite response and tucked the card into the pocket of his suit jacket, knowing he wouldn't call. He wouldn't be up to drinks or anything else after dealing with those kids. Especially after his overnight absence. God only knew what they'd gotten into while on their own. At least he'd had the foresight to have his pal on the police force, Joe Stone, regularly check the house during his absence, thereby guaranteeing that the entire adolescent population of Sioux Falls would not have been partying there.

He remembered that first fateful time he'd gone away on an overnight business trip, not long after the kids' arrival. He had naively expected them to carry on as if he were home. Oh, they'd carried on, all right. His house had been the sight of a teen saturnalia that would have done the ancient Romans proud. The two little guys, Trent and Tony, had their own fun, as well, inventing in-the-house versions of baseball, football, hockey and golf. Never mind pesky obstacles such as lamps and windows that happened to get in the way of a flying ball or puck and break into pieces.

Once again, thinking about the kids had supplanted thoughts of anything or anyone else, he realized. Already, the willing and ready Lorna Larson had been relegated to the realm of forgotten in his mind.

Rafe picked up his car in the parking lot. While driving on Interstate 90 toward home, the urge to keep going—all the way to the west coast without turning around—struck him hard. It was a tempting notion indeed.

But his sense of duty and responsibility was stronger than his longing for freedom. Rafe Paradise headed home.

"We're gettin' new neighbors and it's gonna be cool. Maybe there's a kid and he'll go to our school. We can play golf an——" Ten-year-old Trent paused in the middle of the rap song he was composing. "What rhymes with golf?" He kept up his beat, hitting the edge of the coffee table with two wooden rulers.

"Nothing rhymes with golf," said Kaylin, sixteen. "Why don't you try another word? Like ball. Lots of things rhyme with ball. Call, fall, mall, tall."

"Stop! I feel like I'm trapped in a Dr. Seuss book." Seventeen-year-old Camryn, lying prone on the sofa, adjusted the ice bag on her forehead. "Trent, will you *puh-leese* quit that pounding! Every beat feels like a nail being driven into my head."

"Call me Lion," demanded Trent. "Did you get drunk again last night, Camryn?"

"Like I'd ever tell *you!* You'd run straight to Rafe and squeal on me, you weaselly little tattletale." Camryn heaved a groan. "Kaylin, get me a couple Excedrin. And a cola. And some ice cream."

"Sure." Kaylin scurried into the kitchen to do her sister's bidding.

"She's not your slave, y'know," Trent declared. "Slavery is against the law."

"So is murder, but if you don't stop making so much noise, I'm going to kill you," Camryn warned.

Trent resumed his ruler beat, this time with a new rap. "I'm not scared of Camryn, even though she's mean. She's ugly, too, so bad she'll make you scream."

Camryn threw the ice bag at him and he deftly dodged it, laughing. Unfortunately, the ice bag hit the overweight mixed-breed dog dozing in the patch of sunlight in the middle of the room. The dog awoke and began to bark.

"Aw, poor Hot Dog." Trent tried to comfort the animal by patting its head. Hot Dog snapped at him.

Trent quickly pulled his hand back. "How come Hot Dog hates me?"

"He doesn't hate you, he's just grouchy when he wakes up," said Camryn. "C'mon, Hot Dog. Come here, sweetie. I'm sorry, I didn't mean to hit you."

"Yeah, she wanted to smack *me*, not you, boy." Trent attempted to pat Hot Dog again. The dog bared his teeth and growled at him. "Y'know, he's grouchy all the time, not just when he wakes up."

"That's 'cause he hates it here," explained Camryn. "He liked living in Las Vegas. Me, too. Of course, who wouldn't like Las Vegas better than Sioux Falls?"

"Me!" crowed Trent. "I love Sioux Falls."

"That's because you and your little brother have been stuck here all your lives. You can't compare it to anything else." Camryn heaved a long-suffering sigh. "Hey, where is that kid, anyway? Why isn't he here making my headache even worse?"

"Tony slept over at the Steens' last night. They're going to the zoo today, they said we could both come along, too. Hey, know what, Camryn? When I'm as good a golfer as Tiger Woods I'll go lots of places besides Sioux Falls," Trent vowed. "I'll go to Las Vegas."

"And you'll probably blow all your golf tournament winnings in the slot machines. All five dollars of it." Camryn snickered at her own joke.

"I think that Trent is going to be a great golfer." Kaylin rejoined them with Camryn's order. "He'll be the next Tiger Woods. Maybe even better."

Trent beamed. "I'll buy a big house in Las Vegas and you can live there, Kaylin. It'll be a mansion and we can all live there, me and you and Tony and Camryn and Rafe and Hot Dog. And my mom, too, if she wants to."

"What about Flint? And Eva?" Camryn sat up to swallow the pills with a gulp of cola from the can. "Are they going to be living in the mansion with us, too?"

"No." Trent shook his head decisively. "Flint will want to stay here and work and Eva—"

"Wouldn't live with us if you paid her to," Camryn finished for him. "She hates us too much."

"Wonder why?" Trent looked glum. "Wish she didn't."

"If pigs were wishes, we could fly." Kaylin shrugged philosophically. "Or something like that."

A few minutes later Rafe Paradise walked into his living room to find Camryn breakfasting on cola and strawberry ice cream and Kaylin in his chair, a massive blue recliner. She was cuddling Hot Dog, the fattest, homeliest, worst-tempered beast Rafe had ever had the misfortune of meeting. Now he lived with the creature. And Hot Dog, with his imperious sense of canine entitlement, was drooling on the chair's textured upholstery as well as shedding all over it.

Young Trent was stretched out on the floor on his stomach watching TV. Not quality children's programming, Rafe noted dourly, but a poorly drawn cartoon that featured stick figures blasting other stick figures with some version of nuclear weaponry.

Rafe hardly knew where to begin. Since Trent jumped to his feet and ran to greet him joyously, Rafe decided to let the issue of violent cartoons slide—for now. Trent stopped just a few inches in front of Rafe, his arms at his sides, and beamed. A hug would've seemed natural to some, but Trent was wary of physical contact, and Rafe hadn't been raised to be physically demonstrative. So the two smiled their mutual affection.

"Hi, Rafe. Did you have a good trip?" asked Kaylin.

Since she was the one sitting in his chair, Rafe didn't scold her about the dog's presence there, though it was strictly forbidden. Undoubtedly, it had been bratty Camryn who'd placed the offensive Hot Dog in his chair, anyway.

"The trip went well," Rafe replied. His specialty was contracts law, and he knew the details of his work would bore the kids, should he attempt to explain it. So far, he never had.

He zeroed in on Camryn, who hadn't acknowledged his presence at all. She was pouring cola over the ice cream and mashing it into a fizzing mess with her spoon before gobbling it down. At ten o'clock in the morning!

Rafe grimaced. "What kind of a breakfast is that?"

"It's the only breakfast I want," retorted Camryn

"And it's not good for you. I went food shopping before I left for Minneapolis and I know we have juice and eggs and—''

"Quit it, Rafe!" Camryn made a gagging gesture. "You're trying to make me sick on purpose."

"I'll have some juice and eggs, Rafe," said Trent. "I want the kind with the egg fried in the middle of the bread, like my mom makes sometimes."

Rafe looked at him blankly. He had no idea what kind of eggs Trent's mother sometimes made.

"I know what he means. I'll make it for him." Kaylin rose to her feet and headed out of the room. "Anybody else want anything?" she called over her shoulder.

"No thanks." Rafe was grateful for her willingness to help. Kaylin was usually cheerful and cooperative around the house, quite different from Camryn, whose disposition could and often did border on the demonic. But although Kaylin was easier to live with, she was as determined as her sister to run wild with the wrong crowd.

Rafe's temples began to throb. "Did the girls go out last night, Lion?" He never forgot Trent's nickname-of-the-moment.

"I don't know," Trent replied. "I was playing with my Gameboy. It's the best present I ever got, Rafe. Thanks again."

Rafe got the picture right away. The kid wasn't going to squeal on Kaylin and Camryn, maybe his own choice, maybe because they'd threatened him to keep quiet. Perhaps if he rephrased the question, a standard lawyer's trick... "What time did the girls get in last night, Lion?"

"I don't know anything, I was playing with my Gameboy." Trent stuck to his story.

"By the way, Tony is at the Steens'," Camryn said in the acidly sweet tone she used to induce guilt. "Did you forget about him? 'Cause you didn't mention him."

Rafe felt guilty, all right. "I was just about to ask where Tony was." He hadn't forgotten about eight-year-old Tony, he assured himself. He'd been just a second or two away from noticing the child's absence.

As he glanced from the boy to the girls and then to the dog, a peculiar feeling of unreality swept over him. It had been a whole year, and sometimes he still had difficulty believing that they were all here, living with him. That the life he'd known as a carefree bachelor had been so drastically, irrevocably, changed.

"The new neighbors are moving in today," Trent said, flopping back down on the floor. "Did you see the moving truck when you came in, Rafe?"

"No, it wasn't there." Rafe already pitied the new neighbors who'd been unlucky enough to rent or buy the other half of the duplex in this development of town house condominiums. He knew that the kids' noise and other antics had driven the Lamberts, the yuppie couple who'd previously lived there, to move across town.

"Maybe it just pulled in this second. I'm gonna go check." Trent leaped to his feet and ran out the front door, closing it with a jarring slam.

Camryn clutched her head with her hands. "That felt like a cannon blast to the brain," she complained.

"Where did you go last night and what time did you get in?" Rafe forced himself to ask, hating his role as warden. It was a role thrust upon him and he knew he wasn't very good at it.

"I went miniature golfing with my friends and then we stopped at the Dairy Queen for sundaes. Real wholesome Midwest teen fun, huh, Rafe? Oh, and I was home before my curfew." Camryn had a smile that was positively angelic.

Rafe had been fooled by her the first few days after she'd moved in. Then he'd caught on—the girl was actually the devil in disguise.

"Yeah, sure," he said, scoffing his disbelief. "And Kaylin is going to be the valedictorian in her class and you're going to be the prom queen in yours."

The odds of either event occurring went far beyond the realm of possibility, with Kaylin's and her "what's bad about a D?" philosophy toward education and Camryn's Princess of Darkness persona so at odds with the wholesome students at Riverview High. The same odds applied to Camryn's version of how she'd spent her evening.

Kaylin came into the room carrying a plate with eggs and toast and a glass of orange juice. "Where's Trent?"

"Pestering the new people next door, or trying to." Camryn glanced at the food and sat up. "I'm starving! Can I have that?"

"It's Trent's," Rafe said.

"I'll make him some more. It'll be cold by the time he gets back, anyway." Kaylin handed the food and juice to her sister and sat down on Rafe's designer recliner, wriggling in next to Hot Dog. The dog opened one eye, then closed it again, accepting her presence without protest.

"I feel kind of sick." Kaylin swallowed visibly. "Like I might throw up. Maybe I shouldn't have eaten all those Oreos. 'Specially not on top of the Twizzlers."

"For breakfast?" Rafe heaved a groan.

"I had milk with them." Kaylin was defensive. "Milk's good for you."

"Just don't puke in here or else I will, too!" Camryn shuddered as she proceeded to shovel the food into her mouth.

Rafe decided to skip this particular conversation. "I'm going upstairs to unpack and change." He fled from the room.

Two

The moment Holly pulled her overpacked Chevy Cavalier into the driveway of 101 Deer Trail Lane, a young boy came running across the front yard to meet her.

"I'm Lion," he announced as she climbed out of the car. "I live right next door." He pointed his finger. "See, our places are connected. If me and my brother pound on the walls, you can hear us real good."

He seemed pleased by this fact. Holly wondered, a little apprehensively, why and how often the brothers pounded on the adjoining walls.

"Me and Tony—that's my brother—can do Morse code," Lion continued, his eyes bright with enthusiasm. "Not only SOS, either. *All* the letters!"

"That must have taken a lot of practice," Holly said politely.

"Yeah. We'll teach you and then we can send messages. What's your name?"

"Holly."

"Can I call you that? Or are you Mrs. Somebody?"

"You can call me Holly. I'm not Mrs. Anybody." How ironic,

to be quizzed on her marital status moments after setting foot in her new neighborhood. Was this child an agent of her mother's?

Holly smiled and tried to appear more enthusiastic than she currently felt. The exhaustion from the long drive was seeping through her, and the prospect of learning Morse code by pounding on her walls did not enchant her. She felt hungry, stiff, and more than a little frustrated that she wouldn't be able to move in today as planned.

Lion brandished a golf club like a sword while he chattered on. Holly tried to listen, to respond to his many questions, but her head was still ringing with all the directions and suggestions provided by the friendly real estate agent, who had just given her the keys to her rented duplex town house... Along with the unwelcome news that the moving truck had been delayed and wouldn't be arriving with her furniture and other household essentials until sometime tomorrow.

Hopefully, the truck would arrive tomorrow. The agent's perky parting comment, "You know how it goes with moving, there aren't any guaranteed timetables," didn't offer a whole lot of reassurance.

"Watch my chip shot!" exclaimed Lion, placing a golf ball on a wooden tee in the grass along the edge of the driveway.

Holly watched as he whacked the ball with surprising strength. As it sailed through the air, she noticed that an obstacle—her new home—stood directly in the ball's path. Inevitably, a split second later the ball crashed through a window, shattering it.

"I hate it when that happens!" Lion sounded aggrieved. "How come glass always busts like that?"

Holly stared resignedly at the smashed window. "You have a powerful swing, Lion. But you really ought to practice your chip shots at a golf course or a driving range. In fact, it's probably a good idea to practice all your shots there."

"Yeah, that's what Rafe says, too." Lion sighed.

"Trent, I heard glass break." A deep adult male voice sounded behind her.

Holly turned around to see a very tall, dark-haired man in jeans, moccasins, and a white T-shirt approaching them.

"Uh-oh. That's Rafe." The boy lowered his voice to an urgent whisper. "Would you tell him that you broke the window?" He shoved the golf club into Holly's hand. "And can I go get my ball while you're telling him?"

Rafe joined them before any escape could be attempted. He stared from the broken window, to the boy, and finally at Holly, holding the golf club in her hand. "Welcome to the neighborhood." There was a wealth of subtext in his tone. "I'm Rafe Paradise."

It struck Holly as strange that his name was Paradise while his cryptic "welcome to the neighborhood" sounded more like a warning heard at the gates of hell. Or maybe she was simply delirious from all the driving.

Nevertheless, she attempted to maintain conventional etiquette. "Thank you. I'm Holly Casale. Uh, from Michigan."

"She loves golf!" Trent exclaimed winsomely. "Her chip shot is awesome!"

"Give me a break, Trent, I know you broke her window." Rafe took the golf club from Holly's hand. "Now, how are we going to arrange to pay for it?"

"You're mad at me!" wailed Trent. "You hate me! You're going to send me away, I just know it!" Howling at the top of his lungs, he raced down the street.

Holly was nonplussed. "Should you go after him? Is he running away?"

"No, he has nowhere else to go and he knows it. Trent's mother would send him back if he tried to go to her place. Looks like he's heading for the Steens', who truly take the concept of neighborliness to the highest level."

They both watched the boy run to the front door of one of the condos halfway down the block. The door was opened by a woman who greeted Trent with a smile and allowed him to enter.

"Yeah, the Steens." Relieved, Rafe nodded his approval. "God bless them." He shifted the golf club from one hand to the other. "I want Trent to accept responsibility for breaking your window. How about if he cuts your grass for the rest of the summer? Of course, I'll assume the expense of replacing your window."

"I'm confused about something." Holly glanced up at him. He

towered over her, something that rarely happened at her five-foot-eight height. But Rafe Paradise was at least six foot four, and he was definitely towering.

"You have a perfect right to be." His dark eyes glinted. "Feel free to ask whatever question that needs answering."

"The little boy called himself Lion. You call him Trent."

"He's been Lion for the past few months, since he decided to be a golf phenom like Tiger Woods. But his real name is Trent Krider. He's my Little Brother."

"Oh." Holly was embarrassed to hear how astonished she sounded.

The astute Rafe Paradise reacted immediately. "Think capital letters. Trent is assigned to me by the Big Brother/Big Sister organization. Does that satisfactorily explain how a blond, blue-eyed child could be brothers with a half-breed Indian?"

Holly's face turned scarlet. As if of their own volition, her eyes dropped to his well-worn moccasins.

Rafe noticed that, too. "They were handed down to me by my great-great-grandfather, Chief Lightning Bolt, who once ruled the Plains," he drawled. "Being August, it's too hot to wear my buffalo skins, but I keep them and my headdress in the wigwam out back."

Holly was aghast. She had unwittingly insulted him and his proud ancestors!

"I—I never meant to imply...or...or...to—to disparage your Native American heritage in any way, Mr. Paradise. I apologize. I—I never intended to be so tactless and I am deeply sorry that—"

"All you said was 'oh,'" Rafe said dryly. "How was that tactless or disparaging?"

"I was nonverbally disrespectful," Holly lamented, horrified by her lapse. She would not spare herself. "I—I looked at your moccasins."

"Since when is that a crime?"

"Tone of voice, staring, or even silence can be offending and offensive," Holly persisted frantically.

"I was just kidding, okay? Trying to make a joke, although judging by your reaction, I obviously didn't succeed."

Holly wasn't sure how to respond.

"Look, I don't feel offended." Rafe shrugged.

"You are very understanding, Mr. Paradise."

"It's Rafe. We might as well dispense with formalities since we'll be living next door—and my Little Brother has already started breaking your things."

"Accidents happen." Holly smiled at him. "Don't worry about it."

Rafe stared at her. Suddenly, incredibly, he felt as if fireworks were exploding in his head. That smile of hers affected him viscerally. He had to remind himself to breathe as a fierce jolt of sexual desire blasted through him.

Why? How? Rafe was astonished by his unexpected, involuntary response. He didn't believe in the fairy tale of love at first sight; actually, he'd never even experienced a bona fide case of lust at first sight. Attraction, certainly. But to become firmly, achingly hard by simply looking at a woman he didn't know? That had never happened to him before, not even when perusing certain magazines as a curious youth.

Yet he had attained that state right now by looking at the smiling, unsuspecting, and totally unaware Holly Casale. At thirty-two, his adolescence long past, it was disconcerting, not to mention humiliating, to experience a rush of sensual urgency—in public!

Rafe thought of Lorna Larson's determined campaign to engage his attention on the plane earlier today. Nothing she had seductively implied, said or done had inspired even a sensual twinge in him. But here he stood in the driveway beside Holly—who had done nothing at all to try to turn him on—feeling his jeans become uncomfortably tight from his arousal. He hoped to heaven she didn't notice.

She didn't. It should have been a relief to see that she was staring rather bleakly at her car, jam-packed with possessions, the driver's seat the only empty space within. Instead, Rafe felt irked. She was anticipating the tedious job of unloading her car while he burned with desire!

"Well, I guess I'll start unpacking," Holly said, walking toward her car. "Nice to meet you, Rafe."

"Do you need help unloading your car?" Rafe trailed after her like Hot Dog following someone with a doughnut. His offer was an antidote as much as a wish to help out. There was nothing like prosaic physical labor to quash passion.

"I sure do!" Holly smiled again.

Rafe stopped in his tracks, his eyes riveted to her once more. To her slim figure with soft curves and long legs accentuated by tan shorts and a sky blue T-shirt tucked neatly inside the waistband of her shorts. Her complexion had an iridescent ivory glow and her hair, a rich brunette shade, was thick and curly and tumbled nearly to her shoulders. He gazed at her dainty features; her wide-set brown eyes and well-shaped generous mouth were particularly riveting.

And while he studied her, she was opening both doors of her car to more easily unpack it. Rafe shook his head. He wanted her, but she didn't seem aware of him at all. What a stupid predicament!

Get your ego in check! Rafe commanded himself. For all he knew, Holly Casale was happily married with eyes for no other man but her husband. Which made his sharp sudden desire for her even more unseemly.

His lack of female companionship of late was finally taking its toll on him, Rafe decided grimly. When he began lusting after strangers and begrudging their lack of response, it was definitely time to resume dating, however daunting the logistics. He tried to remember where he'd put Lorna Larson's business card. The trash compactor in the kitchen? The wastebasket in his bathroom?

"Trent says he lives here," Holly said conversationally as she reached into the car for her canvas overnight bag.

"That's right. His little brother Tony does, too." Rafe watched the material of her shorts hug the sweetly rounded curve of her bottom as she bent to lean inside the car. His mouth went dry.

"Your Little Brother and his little brother both live with you? How did that happen?" Holly was curious. "I know it's not usually the case in the Big and Little Brother program."

Even her voice was sexy, Rafe thought dazedly, unable to tear his eyes away from her. Her soft husky tones managed to sound both soothing and stimulating, an unexpectedly arousing paradox.

He looked at her left hand clutching her bag, at her long elegant fingers, the rounded nails painted with pale pink polish. She was not wearing a wedding ring or an engagement ring. Rafe found himself fantasizing about her lovely, ringless hand doing all sorts of things...

He forgot what she'd asked him, what they were talking about.

"I was a Big Sister when I lived in Ann Arbor," Holly continued chattily, grabbing a black bag with her other hand. "It was a nice break from the craziness and pressure of med school and my residency. My Little Sister, Stephanie, is all grown up now, but we plan to stay in touch."

Rafe's eyes darted to her black bag, the traditional physician's bag. And she'd mentioned med school. His jaw dropped. "You're a *doctor?*"

"And you're incredulous that I am. Should I be insulted?"

"You look too young to be a doctor. And way too pretty," Rafe said bluntly. He gathered a huge pile of clothing on hangers into his arms.

"These days everybody pretty much accepts the idea of women doctors," she said dryly.

They walked side by side to the front door of her condo.

"I accept the idea of women doctors," Rafe said in defense of himself. "What I said was that you looked too young and pretty to be one."

Holly rolled her eyes. "That kind of pseudo-compliment is impossible to respond to."

"It wasn't a compliment, pseudo or otherwise, it was simply an observation. I have nothing against women doctors. In fact my little sister is in her third year of med school right here in Sioux Falls, and doing really well, too."

"Does she look young? And *pretty?*"

"Touché, Doc." Rafe conceded her point with a chuckle. "Yes, to both questions. Eva is young and pretty and very capable."

Holly inserted her key in the lock and opened the front door.

Rafe followed her into the empty condo and glanced around. "It's the mirror image of my place." He thought of the gang inhabiting his half of the duplex, the kids, the dog. "But a lot neater. Certainly quieter."

Holly set down her bags on the floor of the L-shaped living room and fixed her gaze upon one long wall. "That must be the adjoining wall Trent said he and his brother use to pound out messages in Morse code."

"And you wondered why the real estate agent was so eager to give you such a great price on this place."

He guffawed rather slyly, Holly thought. He was kidding again, right? "I'm renting, with an option to buy," she hedged.

"So you have a safe out. A wise choice." Rafe peered at her from around the mountain of clothes he was holding. "Where do you want me to put these?"

He watched her. She was all huge eyes and translucent skin and long, long legs. Much to his consternation, he remained in a state of acute arousal despite hauling a hundred pounds of clothing. But he obviously conjured up no sexual interest in her.

Rafe groaned.

Holly reacted at once. "Oh, I'm so sorry! Here I am rambling on, and you're standing there with that cumbersome load."

She'd completely misinterpreted his tortured groan. If she only knew! Rafe was torn between laughing and groaning once again.

He did neither.

"I guess the clothes should go upstairs in my bedroom." Swiftly, Holly led the way up the narrow staircase to the largest of the three bedrooms.

On the other side of the inner wall was the wall of his own bedroom. Rafe tried not to think about how close—the proverbial so near yet so far—he would be to her when he was in his bed and she was in hers. Without waiting for further instruction, he dropped the hangers over the steel rod in the closet. The clothes swung wildly.

"Thank you so much," exclaimed Holly. "I know how heavy those—"

"Don't thank me yet. There's still most of your car to unload. When does the rest of your stuff get here?"

"According to Mrs. Yoder, the agent who took the message from the moving company, hopefully tomorrow."

Rafe rubbed his jaw. "Anytime I hear 'hopefully' I fear the worst. Expect that truck to show up sometime next month."

"I thought the same thing. Fortunately, I brought some basic necessities with me in my car. Towels, clothes and shoes, some kitchen stuff. It won't be so bad."

"You do have a Pollyanna view of things." He liked that, Rafe decided. It was a refreshing contrast to his own outlook that sometimes bordered on pessimism and gloom. *Often* bordered on pessimism and gloom, he conceded. "Never mind that you might not have a bed or a chair or even a plate to eat from, you're all ready to heal the sick. What's your branch of medicine? Are you joining an established practice or going solo?"

"I'll be with the Widmark family practice. I start on Monday, so I have a few days to get settled in my house—if the truck arrives on schedule. I'm a psychiatrist," she added.

"A shrink?" Rafe was taken aback.

Did shrinks have some kind of secret tricks of the trade to get people to confide their inner thoughts? The idea spooked him.

He looked less than thrilled, Holly noted. She was accustomed to some people's uneasy reaction to her profession and strove to put him at ease. "Don't worry, I don't analyze every word of everyone I meet. I don't go trolling for prospective patients, and I promise not to try to bulldoze you into psychotherapy."

Rafe saw the open friendliness in her expression, the shining warmth of her eyes. He was lusting for a psychiatrist who could probably explain why, tracing his feelings back to the womb or something. Worse, not an iota of sexual tension was evident on her part while it hummed through his body like electricity across the wires.

He ran his hand through his hair, making a few renegade strands stand on end. Though her profession dealt with interpreting dreams and fantasies, the classy, personable Dr. Casale would probably faint from shock if he were to reveal the erotic images chasing through his mind right now. Because she starred in every one of them.

Rafe glanced again at her ringless hand. Not all married women wore wedding rings. And might not a psychiatrist be unconventional enough to do away with defining symbols like rings?

"So when will your husband be joining you?" Not his smooth-est opening, but Rafe gave himself points for being direct. Well, it was worth half a point at least.

"I'm not married," replied Holly.

"Your fiancé, then. Is he moving here with you?"

"I don't have a fiancé."

"How about your boyfriend? A live-in, or are you doing the long-distance bit?"

"I don't have a boyfriend, either." Holly shook her head. "You're beginning to sound like my mother grilling me for in-formation."

"Feel free to grill me right back," he invited.

"I'd better not. You got so nervous when I told you I was a psychiatrist, you'd probably suspect me of diagnosing you if I started to ask questions."

"I'm not nervous. Or married or involved with anyone." Rafe supplied the answers anyway. "Are you in—"

"If you ask me if I'm looking for Mr. Right, I will not be responsible for my actions," she warned lightly.

"Is that what all your mom's grilling is about, finding Mr. Right?" Rafe laughed.

"It's not only my mother. My sister and my aunts and cousins are just as persistent," Holly admitted. "They all love to play matchmaker and so far I've been their only failure."

"You present the ultimate challenge, huh?"

There was a certain note in his voice... Holly was quite per-ceptive when it came to the nuances in tone or language, a ne-cessity in her profession. She comprehended subtext—and knew he wasn't talking about her mother's matchmaking anymore.

Holly lifted her eyes and saw him, really saw him for the first time. She knew there were all sorts of subconscious reasons why she'd remained immune to his striking masculine appeal until this moment. She'd been fatigued from the drive, preoccupied with her new surroundings. Uncertain of his eligibility and unwilling to be attracted to another woman's man?

Bingo. Forget about being tired and preoccupied, now that she knew his status her feminine radar had been fully activated. Holly took in every male detail.

His hair was thick, straight, and black as coal, worn a little longer than the very short, very trendy cuts currently in vogue. He had a long straight nose and well-shaped sensual mouth. His smooth shaven jaw, his skin the color of polished bronze, was strong and firm with high, sculpted cheekbones. And his eyes...

Holly felt herself being drawn into his gaze. He had the most fascinating eyes. Arched by jet-black brows, they were almond-shaped and very dark. Compelling eyes, burning with intelligence.

And something else. Something alluring. Daring.

She pulled her eyes from his, yet her gaze didn't leave him. It lingered on his broad shoulders and muscular arms. He was so tall. Though she'd always tried to reason away such a superficial concern, a man's height mattered to her. She was attracted to tall men; Rafe Paradise fulfilled that requirement quite well.

Where was her mind taking her? An unnerving combination of excitement and alarm tingled through her. Holly tried to shake it off, but a slow heat began to suffuse her, kindling in her midsection and spreading upward to her face and lower, lower— Her heart jumped. This primitive physical reaction was so unlike her. She was not the sort of woman who looked at a man and felt her insides turn to jelly. She was sensible, logical; too much so, according to her family. Far too prone to rational explanations and intellectualizing, also according to them.

But right now, sensible, logical Holly felt the totally irrational urge to run away from Rafe Paradise and the internal chaos he'd incited in her. Suddenly she was as jittery as a shy eighth grader face-to-face with her first big crush. It was appalling!

"I—I'd better go unpack the car." Her voice, breathless and higher than usual, sounded strange to her own ears.

Rafe cocked his head and stared at her. Her cheeks were flushed and she was breathing rapidly. He watched the outline of her breasts rise and fall beneath the sky blue cotton of her shirt.

Holly felt as if he were looking through her, that he could see the riotous confusion taking place within her and was fully aware of his potent effect on her. Maybe he thought she was coming on to him! After all, she'd blatantly revealed the lack of a boyfriend, fiancé, or husband in her life. *She'd let him know that she was single and available!* Mom and the rest of the family cupids would be thrilled. Holly winced.

She fairly raced out of the room and down the stairs. When Rafe joined her outside, resentment shot through her. He had effortlessly accomplished something that no other man in her life had ever done. Rafe Paradise had reduced her—a self-confident, self-assured professional woman—to the level of a quivering adolescent!

"Are you okay?" he asked.

His voice—deep, gravelly, and low, the same voice she'd previously been listening to with no untoward effects—suddenly affected her like a physical caress. Holly shivered.

"Y-yes, I—" she tried to think of something to say. Some excuse to offer for her manic bolt from the house. And couldn't. She felt like an idiot. Maybe she really ought to read *The Rules* to learn some clever quips to disguise this sort of wildly emotional reflex. Not that she expected it to happen to her again—not ever again!

She and Rafe stared at each other for a long moment.

The silence was shattered by the sound of a young, very disdainful voice coming from the vicinity of Holly's car. "Hey, know what? Your music really sucks! I mean, totally."

Startled, Holly and Rafe turned to stare at the teenage girl who was sitting behind the wheel of the Chevy Cavalier, going through the container of compact discs that had kept Holly alert and entertained during her long drive from Michigan.

"Camryn!" Rafe rasped through his teeth. He strode to the car, Holly at his heels.

Camryn continued to riffle through the CDs. "Yuck, what is this crap? *Guys and Dolls, Finnegan's Rainbow, Annie Get Your Gun?* Even you have better stuff than this, Rafe."

"Get out of there right now, Camryn!" Rafe grabbed the girl's arm and yanked her out of the car. "You have no right to—"

"Believe me, I'm sorry I did," Camryn cut in sarcastically. "I'll have nightmares for weeks about what I saw here. The soundtrack from *Brigadoon?* You gotta admit that's scary, Rafe." She stared at Holly, incredulous. "Do you actually listen to that? Or maybe you have your real CDs in those faux covers because—'' Camryn paused, trying to think of a possible reason why anyone would resort to such a scheme.

"Thanks for graciously offering me an out, but no, what you see is what you'll hear," Holly said wryly. She shrugged. "I love Broadway show tunes, maybe because I was in the spring musical every year, from middle school through high school. We put on all those—"

"Oh, God, you were one of those perky, girly types who sings in school musicals and sells candy bars to raise funds for the big class trip!" Camryn accused. She stared at Holly with the horrified revulsion most people reserve for cold-blooded killers.

Holly's eyes swept over the girl, taking in her chopped-off black hair, greasy with styling mousse, bobby pins stuck in at haphazard angles. She wore the definitive punk makeup, anemic white face powder, at least three coats of black mascara, smudged black eye shadow, and ultra-pale lipstick.

Camryn's attire was the urban decay look: black spandex leggings—never mind the August heat—and a tiny black T-shirt that exposed her midriff and most of her stomach. Naturally, she had a belly button ring. Holly would've been surprised if she didn't.

But the ghastly makeup and hacked-up hair couldn't conceal an indisputable fact: Camryn possessed an exotic beauty. Minus the startling diversion of her cosmetics, clothing and hairstyle, her looks would ascend to the traffic-stopping level.

Holly's professional interest was piqued. Why had the teenager chosen to look alarming rather than attractive? There could be any number of reasons, ranging from normal teenage rebellion to a multitude of pathologies.

"Who are you, anyway?" demanded Camryn, still glowering at her.

"I'm moving in—"

Camryn erupted with a disgusted, "Duh!"

Rafe heaved an exasperated sigh. "Holly, this is my half sister Camryn. She and her sister Kaylin live with me. And I apologize for her rudeness because she never will."

"Notice how he said *half* sister." Camryn was sardonic. "Making sure you know that me and my sister are only *half* related to him."

"I did notice that," Holly said quietly.

She'd also noticed that Rafe was eyeing his younger half sister as if she were an alien from some incomprehensible galaxy. She'd seen that same look on the faces of the frazzled relatives of her angry and confused young patients back in Michigan.

"Oh, wow, get ready to apologize to our new neighbor again, Rafe. 'Cause here comes your other *half* sister to embarrass you, too," Camryn taunted as Kaylin emerged from the duplex and walked toward them.

Rafe's lips thinned to a grim straight line. Camryn had scored a direct verbal hit. He'd never realized it before, but he always did refer to the two girls as his half sisters. He always thought of them that way.

His half sisters. Never his little sisters. They'd shared the same father, Ben Paradise, but their mother had not been his. Maybe the fact that he had Eva, whose parents were also his, who had always been his adored "little sister," kept that "half" firmly affixed in regards to Camryn and Kaylin.

Certainly all those years spent apart from the pair made him feel less connected to them. And the big age difference between himself and the girls didn't make things any easier. Nor did their rebellious personalities.

He'd really enjoyed Eva as a teenager. Maybe if Camryn and Kaylin were more like her...but they were the antithesis of Eva. They scorned their older half sister as one of those "perky, girly" types, the same despised category Camryn had just assigned to Holly.

Rafe looked at Holly, saw her glance from Camryn to Kaylin and back to him with the alert intensity of a microbiologist who'd just discovered a new species of pathogens. That flare of sexual awareness he'd seen in her soft brown eyes was gone. Her interest in him now was as a prospective case study. One of the dysfunctional Paradise kin. He conceded they could give an ambitious shrink plenty of material to work with.

"Hey," Kaylin greeted them cheerfully, and returned Holly's welcoming smile with a shy one of her own.

Holly introduced herself.

"I'm Kaylin. Cam's my little big sister." The girl amiably

slung her arm around Camryn's shoulder, and Holly observed the four-inch difference in their height.

Camryn was a petite five-two, thinner and smaller-boned than her younger sister. Kaylin was cute with long, dark, straight hair and bangs. She wore no makeup at all, and was dressed in baggy oversize pants and an equally huge shirt that rendered her completely shapeless.

"You're the big little sister," Camryn amended affectionately. Then she looked back at Holly and Rafe, and her dark eyes flashed with anger. "Wait till you see the sainted Evita. You'll know why Rafe and—"

"Camryn, drop it, okay?" Rafe cut in impatiently. "And since you're both out here, make yourselves useful and help Holly unload her car."

Holly was confused. "*Evita?* You mean the movie? Or the CD soundtrack? I haven't gotten around to purchasing it for my collection."

Camryn and Kaylin looked at each other and snickered. "Evita is no soundtrack—she's Rafe and Flint's wicked sister," explained Camryn. "Not a half one, a whole one."

"That would be Eva, the medical student?" Holly recalled Rafe's mention of her.

It took no special intuitive powers to ascertain that the diminutive used by the girls was not based on fondness. The teens' hostility toward their half sister was palpable.

Kaylin nodded her head. "That's her, Evita the Witch Doctor. And Flint is Rafe's Evil Twin."

"Are you really a twin?" Holly looked at Rafe in genuine surprise. Or were the girls playing word games with her?

"Yes," Rafe muttered.

He wasn't about to deny his own brother, though he guessed what his admission would mean. Studies of twins were highly valued in the fields of both psychology and biology; he and Flint had certainly been invited to take part in enough of them by eager university researchers. As Native American identical male twins, they were coveted as a resource treasure. Rafe scowled. He did not appreciate Holly Casale viewing him as a potential lab rat.

"And Eva is not a wicked witch and Flint is certainly not evil," he added, in defense of his siblings.

He reached inside the car and pulled out Holly's bulging, battered old suitcase that she knew must weigh about eighty pounds. The muscles of his arms rippled as he carried it.

Kaylin pulled out a hanging shoe rack, the compartments stuffed with shoes, and dragged it toward Holly's front door.

Camryn didn't move. "You can see how much Rafe doesn't like us," she said, sensing Holly's interest, watching her stare at Rafe and the suitcase. She smiled her angel smile. "Still, he's the *good* one. When our mom called to tell him she was sick, he promised that Kaylin and me could live with him after she died 'cause there was nobody else. And he came and got us when she did. Flint and Eva wouldn't't've even—"

"Stop stalling and get to work, Camryn," Rafe called, feeling his anger rise.

He never discussed private family matters with anyone. And Holly was a shrink! That was easy to forget when his mind was fogged by her potent allure, but the appearance of his half sisters had cleared his head as effectively as a whiff of old-time smelling salts.

"I don't have to!" yelled Camryn as Rafe lugged the suitcase into the condo. "And I'm not throwing a pity party for myself, either," she added, as if to fend off that particular accusation.

Holly had no intention of making it. "From what I've heard so far, you have every right to." She lay her hand on Camryn's forearm. The girl was trembling. "I'm sorry to hear about your mother's death." Her training and her own natural instincts kicked in; she wanted to interpret and diffuse the rage and discord plaguing this family.

"Our dad is dead, too," Camryn said flatly. "Kaylin and me didn't know him at all. He got divorced from Mom when we were one and two years old and we never saw him again. We didn't see Rafe or the others again, either, not till last year after Mom died."

Holly found the information tragic and disconcerting but was skilled enough not to show it. "You and Kaylin hadn't seen your brothers and sister from the time you were one and two years old until last year?'' she calmly restated the essential facts she'd been told.

Camryn nodded. "And now I'm seventeen and Kaylin is sixteen, so you do the math."

Holly accepted the challenge. "You hadn't seen them in fourteen years."

Which meant Rafe had last seen his half sisters as babies, but had taken in two distinctly individualistic teenagers. No wonder he'd stared at them as if they'd been dropped from outer space!

"Yeah, fourteen years. You're a regular math genius," Camryn drawled. "Color me impressed. But they're our half brothers and half sister, don't forget that. *They* never do."

"Do you sometimes wish they would?" asked Holly.

Before Camryn could answer, Rafe was back, having deposited the suitcase inside the house. "Camryn, it may interest you to know that Dr. Casale here is a psychiatrist."

Camryn's expression was instantly thunderous. "I refuse to talk to any shrink! I'm not crazy."

"No, you're not," agreed Rafe. "Don't let her fool you, Doc. Camryn Paradise is no pitiful Little Orphan Annie. Vampira is closer to the mark."

"What I am is a wild, in-your-face-brat with a bad attitude," Camryn proclaimed. "Right, Rafe?"

"So we've been told." Rafe sucked in his cheeks. "Some have claimed you're the most monstrous brat ever to set foot in the city of Sioux Falls—or maybe the entire state of South Dakota."

"That's exactly what my history teacher said and the music teacher agreed!" Camryn was gleeful. "And how about my French teacher?"

"Let's not get into that." Rafe remembered the scene with the French teacher. It had gotten ugly; Camryn would not be taking French when she started her senior year the day after Labor Day, just a few weeks away.

"Aren't you scared I live next door to you, Dr. Nutburger? You should be! You better not try to trick me into any stealth therapy because I'm capable of anything!" boasted Camryn.

Rafe tried to remember who'd made that last quote—"The little fiend is capable of anything!" The outraged home ec teacher?

The hostile volleyball coach? Everybody in Riverview High had something to say about Camryn. None of it good.

"I'm not afraid of you and I wasn't trying to trick you in any way, Camryn." Holly remained unruffled. "But I am curious as to why both you and your brother are so opposed to the idea of any kind of—"

"Family therapy?" Camryn interjected. She made it sound as appealing as imbibing rat poison.

"So you're familiar with the concept," said Holly. "I wish it had been presented to you as a positive aid instead of a negative threat."

"Forget it, Dr. Headshrinker. I won't talk to you."

"Nobody in the Paradise family has ever gone to a psychiatrist," Rafe added.

"Watch out, Rafe, there are sooo many comebacks to that one!" Camryn was suddenly all smiles again. "She could really zing us good."

Holly wondered if the duo realized they were both on the same side; she doubted that occurred very often. Unfortunately, they were allied against her and her profession. Still, she was accustomed to looking for strengths to work with and for the first time she saw a bond, however tenuous, between Rafe and his little sister. The insight cheered her.

"Too easy. I think I'll pass." Holly grinned.

Rafe found himself staring at her again. When Holly Casale turned on the full force of her smile, her whole face lit up and she was downright irresistible. He swallowed. Incredibly enough, he was starting to get turned on all over again, simply standing there gazing at her.

"Well, I'm not going to help you unpack your car, Dr. Headcase," announced Camryn. "I have other plans."

Rafe wondered if he should demand that she stay and help. He hadn't heard of any plans she'd made for this afternoon—not that he was ever consulted first by either girl. Their modus operandi was to do what they pleased, hope they didn't get caught, and show no remorse if they did.

His eyes met Holly's, and he knew that she knew he was totally at a loss in dealing with his young half sisters. Part of him was angry, the other part relieved. He needed help but was loath to seek it, wasn't sure how and where to look. He guessed that Holly probably knew all that, too.

They both watched Camryn stroll back into Rafe's side of the condo.

"Don't say a word," warned Rafe.

"Who me? I wouldn't dream of it. I already promised I don't troll for prospective patients."

"Even though you think we're a prime collection of basket cases."

"I don't think that at all, I just—"

"Uh-oh, this is awful heavy!" Kaylin called from the car. She had managed to get Holly's television set out of the back seat and stood holding it—while tottering precariously.

"Kaylin, put that down!" commanded Rafe. "It's too heavy for you to carry. I'll get it."

"Okay." Kaylin panted. She swayed backward, rendered off balance by the television's weight, then leaned forward in an attempt to put it down.

Holly and Rafe were both watching at the crucial split second when Kaylin's arm strength completely gave out.

The television set crashed onto the cement driveway.

Three

———

Kaylin burst into tears. "I'm sorry! I didn't do it on purpose! It just fell!"

Rafe picked up the set, which had hit at an angle and then bounced to a facedown landing. The double impact caused the screen to shatter and the back console to split open. Inside parts began to spill out.

"Looks like a gutted trout," he observed grimly.

"Stupid piece of junk!" wailed Kaylin. When Rafe placed the wrecked set upright on the ground, she gave it a furious kick, inflicting even more damage, though it was already plainly irreparable. "It only fell a little way and it broke into a zillion pieces!" She kicked it again. "Crummy old trash!"

"I'm inclined to agree with you." Holly calmly surveyed the wreckage. "They obviously don't make these things good and sturdy like they used to."

Kaylin stopped crying and caught her breath. "Yeah," she agreed, her voice tremulous. "If it was good and sturdy, it wouldn't be so smashed."

"It wouldn't be so smashed if you hadn't dropped it," Rafe noted pointedly. "For crying out loud, Kaylin, you—"

"You're mad at me! You hate me!" Kaylin screamed. "You're going to send me away!" She raced to her own front door and disappeared inside.

Rafe and Holly stood in silence.

"I'm going to take a wild guess that Trent co-opted those heart-rending lines from Kaylin," Holly said dryly. "Both seem to share a penchant for highly dramatic exits."

"They *all* do. And I honestly don't know what to say, Holly." Rafe jammed his hands into his pockets and stared glumly from the smashed television set to the smashed window of her condo. "An apology is hardly adequate, but I am terribly sorry that the kids—"

"Rafe, you don't have to apologize. It's okay. The set was ancient, it was on its last legs, anyway. I have a better one, a newer model, that'll be arriving on the moving truck. Really, it's no big deal."

"It is a big deal," Rafe countered. "Don't try to minimize what's happened, Holly. Things started going wrong from the moment you arrived here—thanks to us, your hellacious next-door neighbors."

Silently, dispiritedly, he ran down the list: Trent and Kaylin breaking her things, Camryn insulting her and her taste in music. And of course, both he and Camryn had heartily disparaged her chosen profession. Mustn't leave that out, he reminded himself.

He shook his head. "You must be ready to—"

"I'm not about to run away screaming," Holly assured him. He looked miserable, and compassion swept through her. "But I am ready to take a break from unpacking and I would love something cold to drink." She gave him her most winning smile, inviting him to make her an offer.

"I'd ask you over but you probably feel like you'd be taking your life in your hands if you dare to step inside my place." Rafe was morose. "And if the possibility of something crashing down on you or into you doesn't scare you, the threat of being in the company of an ogre like me—who sends kids into shrieking paroxysms of terror—should."

"I don't believe for one minute that you're an ogre. What I see are kids who are expressing their insecurities, but the fact that they can verbalize their fears shows they feel enough confidence in their relationship with you to—"

"English, please," Rafe interrupted. "I'm not fluent in shrink-speak."

Holly knew she was not being all that obtuse.

"Simple translation—there are all kinds of families and you and the kids are working to establish your own version. I admire that."

"God knows why! After seeing what you'll be living next to, you should already be in your car, heading for the real estate office to demand another place to rent."

"Hmm, that penchant for high drama must be contagious."

Was she being wry or sarcastic? Her delivery left room for interpretation, and Rafe tried to decide. His eyes narrowed. "Why aren't you heading for the hills, looking for another rental? Why would you consider staying here after—all this?"

Holly looked at him and felt her insides clench, heat pooling deep within her, her breasts tightening. Once again, her sensual response to this man floored her. She almost reached out and touched him; she ached with the need to.

But she didn't dare. He was already suspicious of her. He would probably either assume she was making a pass at him— and she wasn't ready to deal with the consequences of that!—or he would accuse her of applying some sort of touchy-feely therapy.

Holly folded her arms in front of her chest, a defensive gesture to keep her hands from reaching, touching, feeling. "If I was the kind of person who ran away at the first small sign of difficulty, I would have never made it through med school, let alone my psych residency."

"So you're saying that you've dealt with a lot worse than the likes of us?"

Rafe wasn't pleased by her answer. He wasn't sure how he'd expected her to respond but relegating them to the ranks of "bad-but-I've-seen-worse" definitely wasn't what he wanted. Hell, he *knew* what he wanted—her!—but the likelihood of that happening was about as probable as Eva, Camryn and Kaylin going to the Empire Mall together for a jolly sisterly shopping trip.

"I'm saying that I'm moving in next door, come what may." Holly's voice jolted him from his reverie. "And I'm also willing to brave going inside your place for a cold drink—if you ever get around to inviting me in for one."

Rafe shrugged. "Well, you can't say you weren't warned. Let's go in."

He almost reached for her hand; it seemed the natural thing to do. But he caught himself just in time. *Natural?* He really was losing it. He'd just met this woman and he was not the hand-holding type.

He never had been. One of the frequent complaints lodged against him by his girlfriends—back in the days when he'd had the time and energy for girlfriends—had been his reserve. He never indulged in demonstrative little signs of affection like holding hands... But he had almost taken Holly's hand to bring her inside his home.

Instead, he walked briskly ahead of her. She followed at her own pace, making no attempt to match his stride.

Once inside the air-conditioned living room, Holly sat on the sofa and sipped a ginger ale while Rafe opted for his massive blue recliner and a root beer.

"I used to have the genuine stuff." Rafe set his can of root beer in the drink holder built into the arm of his chair. "You know, real ale and beer. But Camryn and Kaylin and their delinquent posse drank every drop in the house one evening when I went to a movie. I never made that mistake again."

"Which mistake?" teased Holly. "Going to the movies? Or leaving alcohol with unsupervised teenagers?"

"Both, actually. Now I wait for movies to come out on video and I only buy soft drinks. What a way to live, huh? My brother thinks I'm nuts." He cast her a droll glance. "Oops, am I allowed to use that word around you?"

"I'm a firm believer in free speech. Say whatever you want."

"I figure we've already offended you enough, Doc. No use adding more trouble to the tab. There'll be plenty of time for that later," he added under his breath.

"I heard that. And I'm not anticipating any trouble."

"Well, you should be. From the time the kids moved in here, not a day went by without a complaint from Craig and Donna Lambert. They're the couple who owned your half of the duplex, the people who couldn't wait to escape from it—and from us."

"Did it ever occur to you that maybe the Lamberts were pathological fault-finders?" Holly leaned forward, her brown eyes earnest. "That they were using their complaints against the kids as a bond between them because their marriage was falling apart and they needed *something* to unite them? But instead of facing their problems and their growing estrangement, they seized the easy way out. They found a convenient scapegoat to blame for everything—the kids next door. In some marriages, parents will choose one of their own children to fulfill the scapegoat role and—"

"Did it ever occur to you that not everything needs to be analyzed, Holly?" Rafe interrupted. "The Lamberts complained every day because they had reason to. Trent and Tony practiced Morse code on the walls in preparation for their career as Navy Seals. They played all kinds of sports right here inside in preparation for whatever pro career they were considering at the moment. That includes yelling, jumping, throwing, and knocking things over. You get the picture."

"I guess there are practical reasons why sports are played outdoors and not inside a duplex," Holly conceded. "Still, as the old saying goes, 'boys will be boys.' Craig Lambert used to be one himself and Donna Lambert was once a teenage girl who should've understood the—"

"As a teenager, Donna Lambert was nothing like Camryn and Kaylin. There's no way she could understand them. Donna showed me her roomful of high school awards and trophies back when we used to be friends in the prekids days. She was a joiner, a high achiever, practically a different species from Camryn and Kaylin."

"Am I to understand that Donna Lambert kept a shrine to her high school career?" Holly frowned thoughtfully.

"Well, I hadn't thought of it as a shrine, but the stuff was impressively displayed. But before you pronounce her an insufferable egotist—''

"Ah! So she was one."

"No! No, she—"

"You just said so, indirectly. Your choice of words was very telling."

"Didn't you promise not to go around analyzing everything you hear? Well, you're doing it, Holly."

"I apologize. But the more I hear about this Lambert couple, the more my sympathies tend to lie with the children. I think they've been unfairly maligned."

"It should be interesting to get your opinion this time next week—after you've walked the figurative mile in the Lamberts' shoes and literally lived in their ex-condo. And I almost forgot to mention Hot Dog, the hound from hell. The girls brought him with them from Nevada, and he barks and howls whenever the spirit moves him. That can be in the middle of the night, and often is."

He stood up and began to restlessly pace the room. "I try to keep a lid on things when I'm here but I'm not always around. I can't be. I have to go to the office, I have to go out of town on business. If the Lamberts were pathological fault-finders, ultimately, we drove them to it."

Holly took a long drink of her ginger ale. He had painted a rather daunting picture of life in the House of Paradise—as well as life in the place connected to it. But she wasn't about to let him unnerve her, she was no whiny wimp to be driven away. She promised herself then and there that she would not be like the Lamberts who protested every noise. Kids made noise, it was just a fact of life. And she'd always loved dogs.

Her eyes focused on the pair of school pictures in cardboard frames sitting atop the large-screen television set. Two little boys. She recognized one, blond, blue-eyed Trent.

"You never did get around to telling me why your Little Brother is living with you," Holly reminded him. "And his little brother, too." She continued to stare quizzically at the pictures.

"Go ahead and ask me if that is Trent's little brother Tony in the picture beside his." Rafe's eyes gleamed. "You know you're dying to."

"Well, I was wondering if the African-American child in the picture is Tony," Holly admitted.

"Yes. Tony and Trent are half brothers, and please spare me any lecture or analysis on my use of the word 'half.' It's a biological fact of life. The boys have the same mother, Tracey Krider, but different fathers. Unfortunately, neither father is in the picture—or even in the state—and Tracey has hooked up with a jerk who doesn't like having other men's kids around."

"So the boys are here with you," Holly said softly.

Rafe sat down on the other end of the sofa. Holly was two cushions away from him. Close enough for him to smell the alluring scent of her spicy perfume mixed with the heady aroma of her skin and sweat—yet too far away for even an accidental touch. A recipe for frustration. He leaned his head against the back of the sofa and closed his eyes. Best not to look at her, best to recite the facts as dispassionately as possible.

"I've been Trent's Big Brother since he was seven. I sort of unofficially inherited Tony a couple years ago when they couldn't place him with a Big Brother of his own. There is such a long waiting list of kids and a shortage of volunteers—"

Rafe shrugged. "But that's another story. The boys often spent weekends and part of their summer vacation with me but when Tracey took up with her current loser boyfriend, Trent and Tony ended up moving in here full-time. Tracey signed over legal guardianship to me. That also coincided with Camryn and Kaylin's arrival."

Holly gazed at Rafe who had taken in those rejected sons of other men. Who had taken in his orphaned kid sisters. True, he seemed somewhat overwhelmed by his four charges but he hadn't backed away from them, he had willingly accepted responsibility. He was a good man in the true, old-fashioned sense of the term.

A giddy rush of emotion surged through her. She wanted to tell him how much she admired him. He had taken four children into his home when so many men she knew wouldn't commit to even tending a houseplant.

But how to say so? Holly felt strangely shy and couldn't seem to find the words, a most unusual situation because communicating was one of her strengths.

Instead, she resorted to more questions. She was very adept at asking questions. "Do the two groups of kids get along together?"

"Yeah. Oh, there are the usual spats, but on the whole, they all hit it off pretty well. In fact, there are times when it's the Gang of Four versus me."

"And their alliance surprises you?" Holly quipped.

It was one question too many. Or maybe it was the way she'd phrased it. Holly watched Rafe's lips curve into a sardonic smirk. He turned his head and opened his eyes to lazily survey her.

"Yeah, Doc, their alliance surprises me. Are you going to explain why the kids are allies? And why I'm surprised? Since you've already evaluated the Lamberts, let's hear your psychological take on the kids and me."

"Sorry." Holly looked sheepish. "A hazard of my profession, I guess."

"Which one? The interviewing or the analyzing? Maybe I should be lying down on the couch while we're talking, huh, Doc?"

Instantly, Rafe felt heat flash through him. He'd been trying to be glib but it had backfired. There was nothing funny about the image of himself lying on the couch—and Holly Casale anywhere within his reach. The suggestion conjured up erotic images that made his dark eyes smolder.

He tensed as a critical part of him grew stiff as a warrior's lance. And there was nothing he could do about it. The more he looked at Holly, the more he wanted to stretch out on the sofa and pull her down on top of him. Or maybe lay her beneath him. Both scenarios were torturously arousing. But he shouldn't, couldn't, wouldn't attempt to enact either one.

Rafe abruptly crossed the room to snatch his can of root beer and chug it down, wishing it were something a lot stronger. Something to render him senseless, to blot out desire and need. His whole body throbbed with it.

Oddly enough, the whole house seemed to be throbbing, too. It took a moment or two for Rafe's deductive reasoning skills to kick back in. No, the walls weren't shaking, but the pulsating drumbeats blasting from the stereo speakers upstairs in the girls' bedroom gave that illusion. Accompanying the boom was the sound of caterwauling that ranked right up there with Hot Dog baying to ambulance sirens. Camryn and Kaylin called it singing, by their favorite rock bands.

Rafe was actually glad for the return trip to reality. At least this was something he could act upon! He strode from the room to stand at the foot of the stairway.

"If I have to tell you two to turn down that noise again, I'm going to confiscate every single compact disc you own and donate them all to the state prison!" he roared up the stairs.

Camryn and Kaylin responded with complaints and some door-slamming but the blaring volume of the music was lowered.

Rafe returned to the living room.

"The state prison?" Holly laughed. "What kind of a threat is that?"

"Probably an unfair one. After all, the prisoners are serving their sentences, it's illegal to inflict additional punishment on them. In fact, the Constitution specifically prohibits it."

"You think having to listen to the girls' CDs constitutes cruel and unusual punishment?" Holly was amused.

"I guess you think I'm a tyrant, huh, Doc?" Rafe eyed his huge blue recliner across the room but stayed where he was, standing beside the sofa. Holly looked up at him, as if trying to gauge his mood.

The way he was feeling, that was no easy task, even for a summa cum laude shrink. "Are you going to accuse me of squelching the girls' creative outlet?" he challenged.

He felt wired and impatient; the temptations and frustrations of the morning converged, making him reckless. The hell with being careful and covert. When was the last time he'd acted on impulse? His brother would probably amend that to "when was the first time?"

Impulsively, Rafe dropped down onto the sofa. This time he didn't put a two-cushion safety zone between them. He sat right next to Holly. "After all, teenagers express themselves through their music, don't they? Although their idea of music strikes me as brain-numbing din. Definitely cruel and unusual punishment for anyone to have to listen to."

"It's not exactly what I'd call the sound of music, either." Holly forced herself to remain in her seat, to project a calm and steady exterior though she felt neither. Rafe had clearly invaded her personal space by sitting so closely to her.

She'd once written a paper on the subtleties of personal space, how it varied from culture to culture, family to family, person to person. But one didn't have to thoroughly research the subject to know that when a man deliberately chose to sit very near a woman, when he leaned toward her, bringing himself so close that their knees touched and their shoulders brushed...

Holly gulped. What now? She twisted her fingers, trying to think. *Always think before you act.* Her own words of wisdom, quoted to so many impulsive adolescents in group therapy, rang in her ears. But how could she think clearly when sensual flames licked at those places where their bodies touched? And in other secret, hidden places where they didn't.

Her self-control fought an internal battle to ignore what she was feeling. And won, sort of.

"I don't think you were being tyrannical." Holly tried hard to stick to the subject they'd been discussing. "After all, the girls needn't express themselves at such ear-damaging decibel levels. As...as the adult in charge, you have the right—no, the obligation—to set reasonable limits. Children need that, they actually want it."

"Yeah, sure." Rafe chuckled quietly. "Go upstairs and ask Camryn and Kaylin how much they want me to tell them to play their music quietly."

He laid his hand on her back, making his invasion of her personal space into a blatant takeover. "On second thought, don't go upstairs. Don't go anywhere at all."

Holly marveled at his ability to render her immobile with that simple husky command. Certainly, it wasn't his hand resting lightly on her back that held her in place; she could've easily shrugged it off and gotten up. But she didn't. Because she didn't want to.

Instead, she found herself swaying into him as his mouth

moved closer to hers, closer...then took a slight detour. His lips skimmed her earlobe, the slender curve of her neck. Deep within her, desire sparked to urgency. Holly trembled as she felt his warm breath against her skin, followed by the gentle touch of his mouth. He was making her ache with need, which was fast building to nerve-racking frustration. He was taking it so slowly, and she wanted more.

Her eyelids fluttered as he tilted her head with his fingers, cupping her chin with his one hand while languorously rubbing her back with the other. "Are you going to tell me to stop?" he murmured.

Holly held his gaze for a long, charged moment. She couldn't ever remember wanting to be kissed as badly as she did at this moment.

"No," she whispered on a sigh.

Her eyes locked on his mouth, his beautiful sensual mouth, and longing swept through her in deep, rolling waves. Holly swallowed hard. This was so unlike her, the urgency, the impulsivity. She didn't go around kissing men she hardly knew, or even wanted to. Why, she could hardly remember the last time she'd been kissed; it had probably been a perfunctory peck after one of those wretched blind dates her family had inflicted on her.

"No?" he repeated. Teasing her. He touched his lips to hers, tempting her, then retreated.

Holly's heart lurched. "Yes," she breathed.

Her hands clutched his shirt, not letting him move away. It didn't occur to her until much later that he hadn't tried to, that while he'd lifted his mouth from hers, his body had moved closer, pressing her back against the sofa cushions. Her breasts were crushed against the satisfying hard warmth of his chest and her nipples tightened into taut little beads.

Rafe smiled a sexy smile and brought his lips back to hers to linger lightly. Holly's eyes snapped shut, and she was instantly swept into a dark vortex of intimacy. She was aware of nothing but him and everything about him. When he kissed her softly again, she clung to him, her senses reeling.

Their lips moved fluidly, lazily, opening to deepen the kisses, to touch tongues in a teasing little duel. Rafe threaded his fingers through her hair, massaging her scalp gently, sensuously. She glided her hands over the soft cotton of his shirt, feeling the muscles of his back strong and warm beneath the cloth. They sank lower, deeper into the sofa, their legs becoming entwined.

"Rafe. Hey, Rafe!"

The sound of the boisterous young voices penetrated their private little world with the potency of a neutron bomb. Rafe sprang to his feet and bolted across the room, practically flinging himself into his recliner. Holly sat up, grasping the arm of the sofa for support. She was shaking so badly she knew she wouldn't be able to stand.

As Trent and Tony burst into the room, she caught a glimpse of the expression on Rafe's face. His face was flushed and he looked as guilty as a kid caught with his hand in the cookie jar; she expected she looked much the same.

Holly fought a wild urge to giggle and was horrified—how inappropriate, how mortifying! She hadn't giggled since junior high, if then.

"The Steens went to the zoo, but we decided to come home and be with you," said Trent.

"I wanted to see you. I missed you, Rafe," exclaimed Tony. "Will you take us to the zoo?"

"Not today," Rafe said reflexively.

His eyes met Holly's across the room, and he could read her mind because he was thinking the same thing. That they were damn lucky it was the boys who'd nearly caught them necking on the sofa because Tony and Trent were too young and too oblivious to be aware of the thick sexual tension between the adults. Camryn and Kaylin would've picked up on it immediately.

"Hi, Holly," Trent chirped, bounding over to her. "She's Holly," he informed his brother. "She's moving in next door."

Tony viewed her with interest. "You got any kids?"

"No." Holly shook her head. The little boy looked so disappointed, she felt obliged to offer him a regretful, "Sorry."

If only Rafe would stop staring at her! He possessed an uncanny ability to unnerve her, a sensation she was not at all accustomed to. *Unnerving you isn't all he does to you*, she forced herself to admit.

"Do you hate kids?" Tony persisted. "The Lamberts did. We hated them right back, too. They were mean!"

"I don't hate kids," Holly assured him.

She shifted slightly, her body still aching with arousal, her mind cloudy. Though she tried to focus on the children, she couldn't keep her eyes away from Rafe. She watched him watching her, saw his intense gaze linger on her lips, which parted as though he'd physically touched them.

His eyes traced her jawline to her neck, to the collar of her shirt where her skin disappeared beneath the smooth cotton of her top. Unable to pull away, they sat tethered in each other's gazes while the boys bounced around the room.

Trent and Tony turned on the television set, they pulled board games from the shelves and unearthed videotapes from a lower cabinet.

"So what do you want to do?" asked Trent, retrieving a basketball from behind the sofa. He tossed it at the wall where it scored a loud thump. "Bull's-eye!" he called eagerly.

"That was no bull's-eye," Tony scoffed. "Anybody can hit a wall. Anybody! Look how big it is—and it doesn't even move."

"Tell him, Rafe!" howled Trent in protest. He threw the basketball at Tony, who deftly dodged it.

"Tell him what? He does have a point, Lion," said Rafe. "Ever think why Hit-the-Wall Ball isn't a sport, or even much of a game? It's just too easy."

Tony reappeared with a soccer ball and kicked it into the wall. "Bull's-eye!" he shouted.

"You said it wasn't a bull's-eye! You said anybody can hit a wall." Trent was indignant. "Rafe said Hit-the-Wall Ball isn't a game or a sport cause it's just too easy."

"I still made a bull's-eye." This time Tony lobbed the basketball at the wall. "And I just made another one."

Holly couldn't suppress her grin.

"You think that's funny, huh?" Rafe stood up. He looked very tall, very strong, and all male. He sauntered across the room toward her. "Wait until you're sitting over there on the other side listening to all those thuds. I doubt that you'll be smiling then."

Rafe stood in front of her, holding out his hand to her. Holly's

pulses pounded crazily as she stared at his big hand, at the muscles of his outstretched arm. It took her a second or two to realize
that he was offering to help her up. Tentatively, she laid her hand
in his.

He hauled her to her feet with one smooth pull. And kept hold
of her hand. Holly felt the strength of his long bronzed fingers,
and a syrupy warmth flowed through her.

"No more throwing balls at the wall, guys," Rafe said to the
boys, his eyes never leaving Holly's. "You're not allowed to
throw or kick balls inside, remember? Take the balls outside and
play with them there."

"Will you play with us, Rafe? Please?" begged Tony.

"I'm going to unload the trunk of Holly's car," said Rafe.
"You two can help if you want."

"I want to help!" cried Trent.

"And get your golf ball back from inside her place," Tony
added knowingly.

Trent's blue eyes darted from Tony to Rafe to Holly. He looked
guilty and defensive and not at all happy about the unpleasant
reminder of the golf ball incident.

Holly's child psych stint during her residency had included
interpretation of children's behavior. She quickly stepped in to
subvert the loud, emotional defense Trent looked ready to stage.

"I know the broken window was an accident...uh, Lion," she
said soothingly. "In fact, Kaylin had an accident this morning,
too. It can happen to anybody. I understand."

"What did Kaylin break?" Tony was immediately intrigued.

"Holly's TV set," Rafe said flatly. "She dropped it."

"Wow! That's a lot worse than busting a window." Trent went
from appearing upset to positively glowing with delight. "Where
is it?"

"Outside in the driveway in all its broken glory," said Rafe.

Without another word, the two boys ran out of the room and
out of the duplex to view the remains.

Holly and Rafe looked at each other. For a moment she thought
he was going to kiss her again. The intent was in his eyes and in
the tension of his body as he turned toward her. And she wanted
him to. Desperately. Never mind the teenage girls upstairs and

the little boys waiting outside in the driveway. At this excruci-ating, exquisite moment in time, there was nobody else in the world but the two of them.

"Are you sure you're ready for this?" Rafe abruptly dropped her hand and moved away from her. His withdrawal was unmis-takable as he headed for the door.

Holly found the question indiscernible. Now freed from his, her hand felt oddly empty. Unattached. Worse, the feeling grew and spread until the sense of disconnection and loneliness had pervaded her entire being. *Because Rafe wasn't holding her hand, because he hadn't kissed her again?*

She followed him outside, deeply shaken. She'd never been given to roller-coaster highs and lows, had always believed herself to be a person whose emotions ran deep but steady. A person of necessary and formidable guard and reserve. But the short time she'd spent with Rafe Paradise had revealed another side of her—a startling, rather alarming side.

Holly thought of the years she had spent loving Devlin Bren-nan, all through med school and their respective residencies. Dur-ing that time, she had remained true to her self-image—calm and steady, in total control. Which was important, it was necessary, because Dev hadn't fallen in love with her. They had been fated to be best friends, and she had settled for that. Certainly, she hadn't turned into a moody depressive because things hadn't worked out exactly as she might've wished.

So why was she feeling so moody and depressed right now? Because Rafe wasn't holding her hand and hadn't kissed her again?

Holly joined Rafe and the boys, who had gathered around the smashed TV set. Trent and Tony admired it greatly. They wanted to ask Kaylin to pick up the set and drop it again, so they could view the action firsthand. Rafe firmly vetoed that plan.

"Open the trunk so we can get started," he ordered Holly, using the same commanding tone.

"Sir, whatever you say, sir!" She'd meant to be funny but her voice betrayed a caustic edge. She marched to the trunk and flung it open.

During the many trips from the car into the condo and back

again, Holly concentrated on the kids, talking to them, joking with them. Completely ignoring Rafe. Of course, he ignored her, too.

By the time the entire car was empty, Holly was Trent and Tony's new best friend. They asked her to take them to the zoo, to the movies, to play ball—and to stay for dinner that evening.

"Give her a break, guys." Rafe finally spoke up. He'd been silent as he carted the heaviest loads, letting Holly and the boys carry the conversational ball along with the easy-to-lift stuff. "She's tired. I'm sure she wants to check into a motel and just sack out."

"Can we go to the motel, too?" asked Tony. "They might have a pool there."

"We like to go to lots of places," explained Trent. "We really like motels with pools in the summer."

"Stop hustling her, kids," warned Rafe.

"Sure, you can swim in the motel pool," Holly countered. "If it's okay with Big Brother, that is."

His look of disapproval shouldn't please her so much, she admonished herself. There was no rational reason why she should want to irritate him...but then, she'd been behaving irrationally since shortly after meeting Rafe Paradise.

"It's okay with you, right, Rafe?" cried Trent.

"Let me talk to her first," said Rafe. "Go play something."

"You can't talk to her if we're not here," argued Tony. "Somebody has to stay and get you to say yes, in case you say no."

"Impeccable logic," Holly agreed.

"You guys go play some one-on-one. You, come with me." Rafe grabbed Holly's hand and pulled her along after him, into her half of the duplex.

His caveman tactics caught her completely off guard. Holly was inside before she rallied her scattered wits to protest. "Just for future reference, I don't appreciate being dragged around like a...a —" She paused seeking a suitable example.

Holly felt light-headed. A repeat adrenaline rush on an empty stomach could affect a person that way—and in other crucial ways, too. Like throwing off her timing.

Her timing was definitely off, Holly realized vaguely. Because before she could shove Rafe away, he had taken her wrists and pinned them at shoulder height to the wall. She jerked her arms but his grip was strong as steel.

"I'm waiting, Holly," Rafe whispered, enunciating every word. "Are you going to berate me for behaving like a differently developed hominid?"

Holly's sense of humor swiftly displaced her outrage. And then her laughter turned into a gasp as he moved the lower part of his body fully, firmly, against her. She felt the pressure of his erection as his mouth nuzzled her neck, gently nipping and kissing.

"Rafe," she whispered shakily. "What are you doing?"

"I don't know," he mumbled, his breathing raspy. "But you want me to do it, don't you?"

She couldn't argue with that. When he released her hands, she slid her arms around his neck, surrendering to him, to her own explosive need, and to the chemistry between them.

His mouth descended on hers, parting her lips with his tongue to kiss her deeply. He moved his hands slowly over her, as if luxuriating in the feel of every curve.

Holly moaned softly. Rafe was right. She wanted this. She wanted him.

Four

She threaded her fingers through his thick black hair as their kiss went on and on, becoming deeper, harder, more demandingly intimate. He seemed to surround her with his sheer male size and strength, making her feel weak and vulnerable, yet more powerfully feminine than she had ever felt in her life.

Her breasts swelled as liquid fire burned a path to her belly and beyond. Holly clung to Rafe as her only anchor as she swirled and spun in the tumultuous wild seas of sensuality.

He muttered something dark and sexy against her mouth when he placed his hand over her breast in a gesture of pure masculine possession. His words, as provocative as his caresses, incited Holly to push herself more firmly into his palm. His thumb glided over the taut bud of her nipple.

She moved against him in erotic rhythm while pleasure spiraled through her. Holly felt a savage shudder pass through him, and into her, as if their bodies were already connected.

Rafe slid one denim-clad thigh between her legs. The roughness of the material against her skin was an added stimulant to her already heightened senses. Holly drew a sharp breath as she tightened her thighs around him.

He increased the pressure as his hands smoothed up and down her legs. Her skin was warm and supple and satiny soft; his fingers kneaded and stroked, but it was not enough. His knuckles brushed the hem of her shorts, and he groaned with frustration.

It was definitely time to remove the maddening impeding barrier. Rafe ran his forefinger around the waistband of her shorts and located the zipper. He was tugging at it when the first boom sounded.

For a moment they were both too caught up in the whirl of passion to pay any attention. They disregarded the next few thuds, too, but the rapid pounding persisted, finally becoming too loud and persistent to ignore. Rafe dropped his hands to his sides. Already his body was taut with an entirely different kind of tension. He uttered a low curse.

Slowly emerging from the sensuous haze engulfing her, Holly realized that her arms were still wrapped around Rafe. She was clinging to him while he stood as still and unyielding as a telephone pole. And just about as responsive.

"What's that noise?" Her voice sounded drowsy and seemed to come from far away. She tried to hold his eyes but he lowered his gaze, looking away from her.

"Morse code," Rafe growled through his teeth. He raised his hands to hers, carefully removing them from his neck. "An SOS."

Holly's return to reality was complete. She quickly sidestepped him to stand out of reach, both his and hers. The series of thuds continued against the wall, but she couldn't make much sense of it.

"This is what you'll be hearing at any given hour of the day or night if I'm not there to stop it. Now do you understand why the Lamberts fled?" Rafe stalked over to the wall and began to pound back.

Holly stood and watched. Listening to him communicate with the boys by banging on the wall didn't seem as strange as it might've several hours ago.

"Is there something wrong over there?" she remembered to ask. "Are they calling for help?"

"Of course not. They're the classic Boys Who Cry Wolf."

"Or in their case, who pound SOS." Holly attempted to inject some humor into the situation.

Rafe did not enjoy her little joke. "I know what this is about. Tony and Trent are tired of waiting. They want me to give the okay so you can get going to the motel pool."

"They said all that in Morse code?" Holly was impressed.

"No." Rafe scowled. "Just SOS. But it wasn't too hard to fill in the rest."

"To read between the knocks, as it were," Holly said drolly.

Rafe gave the wall a final pound that probably shook every picture hanging on his side of it. This time, the boys did not pound back.

The ensuing silence seemed to resound. Holly almost wished the kids would send another SOS because without the noise to distract her, she was forced to face what she'd been doing before it all began.

She had given in to her craving to kiss him—and then some. Her whole body felt scorched with the sensual imprint of his. The feel of his mouth on hers, of his hands caressing her, was seared into her memory. She'd been transported to a sweet heaven she had never imagined to exist—by a man she barely knew!

"Damn it, Holly, what kind of game are you playing?"

"Game? What do you mean?"

"I mean..." His voice trailed off.

He felt dizzy, remembering her in his arms, all soft and trembling with desire. The power of her kisses, the touch and the feel of her, had blindsided him, rendering him senseless, and he still hadn't fully recovered. Every time he looked at her, lust pulsated through him.

"Do you even know what you mean?"

Holly's taunt was fairly mild, compared to some he'd endured, but it struck a nerve. Why did she look so calm and collected? Why was she so coherent when he'd been reduced to a hormonally impaired nitwit? It was past time for him to pull himself together.

"I mean, what you were doing with the kids." Rafe cleared this throat. "Playing at being their pal. Offering to take them swimming. If you're doing it to—"

"I wasn't playing at anything!" Holly cut in, stung. "I have no ulterior motive beyond enjoying their company. I happen to like kids and—"

"Trent and Tony have been let down by adults too many times." It was Rafe's turn to interrupt. "Their mother, Tracey, has had boyfriends who would pay attention to the boys when the whim struck, only to tell them to get lost on another whim. Then Tracey herself dumped them because the current sleazeball in her life doesn't want kids around."

"And you think I would do that? Amuse myself with the children and then betray their friendship if I don't feel like bothering with them?" Holly was torn between hurt and outrage.

"I don't know. Will you? I don't know you. I—" He broke off, watching her skin flush with a surge of hot color. Rafe stared in fascination. He'd never seen anyone blush so thoroughly, and he couldn't help but wonder about the other places of her body, unseen and covered by clothing, where she might also be heated and flushed. Moist and pink. Like her breasts, her belly, her—

"No, you don't know me. And I don't know you, either." Holly's voice ripped through his increasingly erotic fantasy. "Which means what we—what we were doing here was way out of line." She swallowed hard. "And totally out of character for me."

She was heading toward a place Rafe did not wish to go. He didn't care to rehash their hot little interlude nor did he want to analyze it. But she would, he was sure of that. Being a shrink, she would be eager to explore every nuance, to interpret every touch. He rebelled at the very thought.

"We weren't talking about that, we were talking about the kids," he said coolly.

"We weren't talking at all. You were accusing me of using the children to indulge my own selfish whims. I would never do that, but I don't expect you to believe me. After all, you don't know me." Holly opened the door and headed outside.

An excellent offensive strategy, fumed Rafe, because it caused him to go running after her. To chase her. And he did, like a hungry wolf intent on its fleeing prey—or even worse, like a conditioned lab rat scenting cheese at the end of some maze.

Oh, yes, she was a skilled tactician; Rafe was thoroughly disgruntled. No doubt her studies and training in human behavior had clued her in to the best ways to manage and manipulate men.

Yet it didn't seem to matter that he had it all figured out. He still chased after her.

As Holly strode toward her car, Rafe's eyes compulsively swept the shapely length of her legs—which triggered another acute sensual memory. He could almost feel the smoothness of her skin, the exciting strength of her firm feminine muscles under his stroking hands.

His imagination abruptly lurched into the X-rated range. He pictured the two of them together, her long beautiful legs wrapped around him, drawing him deeper into her as they soared to a rapturous climax. Aroused and aching, he knew that being imaginary lovers wasn't going to be enough for him. He wanted to experience, not merely to imagine, that scene. His heartbeat, already heavy and fast, roared in his ears.

Rafe was so distracted by the seductive pictures playing in his mind's eye that he didn't notice the empty space in the wide double driveway, where his car, a dark green Jeep Grand Cherokee, had been parked.

But Holly did. "Where's your car?" Its absence caught her by surprise, and she stopped, momentarily diverted from her own escape.

Rafe stared at the empty space, the place where his Jeep should be. The place where he'd parked it upon his return from the airport. Slowly, grimly, comprehension beginning to dawn.

"No, it can't be." He spoke his thoughts out loud. "They didn't!" Except they had, of course. "Those little monsters stole my car!"

Holly folded her arms in front of her chest, a classic defensive position she didn't bother to analyze. "There's that Paradise penchant for high drama rearing its ugly head again. You sound like Stanley Kowalski bellowing for Stella."

Rafe shot her a dark look. "I am not being dramatic. I'm infuriated and I have every right to be."

Trent and Tony came running outside, each clutching a gym bag. "We're ready to go swimming," Tony called cheerfully.

"Did you two know that Camryn and Kaylin took my car?" demanded Rafe.

"Sure," said Trent. "We tried telling you, too. You got our SOS."

"And you told us to shut up," Tony added, "so we thought you didn't care they were taking it."

"That was the reason for the SOS? You were alerting me that the girls were taking the car?" Rafe frowned. "I thought you were getting tired of waiting to go swimming."

"Well, we were," Tony admitted. "But that wasn't worth an SOS."

"You responded to their SOS by pounding 'shut up' in Morse code?" Holly arched her brows at Rafe. "Charming."

"I didn't say 'shut up,'" Rafe snapped. "I told them to stop with the SOS."

"That kinda means shut up," Trent noted. "Camryn said she was bored and since you could use Holly's car, she might as well have yours. So her and Kaylin got your keys and left."

"She and Kaylin." Holly reflexively corrected the little boy's pronoun usage.

"Yeah, both of them," agreed Trent. He didn't realize that she was correcting his grammar. "But Camryn was driving."

Without another word, Rafe walked swiftly into his half of the duplex, leaving Holly and the two boys standing in the driveway.

"Rafe hates it when they drive his car," explained Trent. "Even when he lets them, they're supposed to ask permission and say where they're going and get a curfew and all that."

"I bet that goes over big," murmured Holly, envisioning the scene.

Trent chuckled. "Not!"

"Let's go swimming!" Growing bored with the conversation, Tony tossed his gym bag into Holly's car and scrambled in after it.

Holly heaved a sigh. This was getting complicated. She

couldn't simply drive off with the children when their legal guardian hadn't actually given his permission. In his current foul mood, Rafe might file kidnapping charges against her if she dared to take off with the kids!

Now who was being dramatic? Holly chided herself. "We'd better go inside and ask Rafe if it's okay to leave now," she said, her sound and sensible self again.

"Rafe really, really wants us to go swimming with you," Trent assured her.

"Perhaps. But I have to hear him say so." Holly half expected a tantrum of some kind, but both boys accepted her decision and raced into the house. She followed automatically.

Rafe was in the kitchen on the phone, and the boys headed to the refrigerator to treat themselves to Popsicles from the freezer.

"They won't answer the phone," Rafe stormed. "Well, I can wait them out. I'll stay on the line until they can't stand the ringing and pick up just to make it stop."

"He's calling the car phone," Tony told Holly between bites of cherry Popsicle. He boosted himself up onto the counter and sat there absently swinging his feet, kicking the lower cabinets.

"They usually don't answer when Rafe calls the car phone." Trent hopped onto the counter opposite his brother. "They turn up the CD player real loud so they don't hear it ring so much."

Holly imagined driving a car with the volume of music cranked up to the loudest possible decibel level while the phone rang incessantly. It made her long solitary trip from Michigan with show tunes playing in the background seem heavenly in comparison.

"I'm not giving up," Rafe vowed, staying on the line. The long cord permitted him to pace the kitchen and beyond.

"Wonder if they'll go in the river," mused Tony. "Even though it's hot out today, that water sure is cold!"

"They'd better not go near the river!" Rafe's expression instantly changed from anger to concern. "Neither one of them can swim worth a damn—er, darn. Boys, be honest with me, this is very important. Did the girls say they were going swimming in the river?"

"I'm not a weaselly little tattletale," Trent proclaimed. "Or a squealing little rat, either."

"It isn't considered squealing when there is danger involved," Holly interjected.

She stood in front of Trent, trying to make eye contact with the boy. He skillfully evaded her attempt to optically connect with him. "If Camryn and Kaylin plan to go in the river, their lives are definitely in danger. They could very easily drown," she added.

Trent shrugged. "They won't drown. Sam, Grable, and Becker are going with them. They're huge!"

"It doesn't matter how big or strong anybody is. Swimming in a river is very different from being in a pool with lifeguards," Holly continued. "If the girls can't swim very well, the river is a treacherous place for them to be."

She turned to Tony who'd stopped kicking and appeared to be listening. And though she normally did not approve of manipulating children, she found herself resorting to exactly that. "And, of course, we can't go swimming in the motel pool until the girls are safely found. We certainly don't dare have any fun while Camryn and Kaylin are in danger."

"They said they're going to the river to go swimming," Tony blurted.

"Weaselly little tattletale!" Trent jeered. "Squealing little rat!"

"Tony cares about Camryn and Kaylin and wants to help them," countered Holly. "In my eyes, that makes him a hero." Whose altruism had been boosted by his desire to swim in the motel pool, but she didn't bother to add that. The little boy was beaming proudly.

"Did they say what part of the river?" Rafe asked, continuing to pace the floor while still clutching the receiver. His eyes met Holly's. "The Big Sioux River flows for miles and of course, there is the falls..." He inhaled sharply. "Unless we have some idea where they're headed, we could be driving around for—"

"They'll prob'ly go to that place they like," Tony said brightly. "But I can't remember where it is. It was practically dark when Camryn took us there."

"Camryn took you to the river at night?" Now Rafe was truly aghast.

"Yeah, one time—no, two times," Trent confirmed. "It was a couple weeks ago. You were away on a business trip and she was baby-sitting us."

"She and her friends were having a river party and they really had fun. Me and Trent did, too." Tony grinned. "Hey, Trent, remember our rock throwing contest? You were Ken Griffey Jr. and you won."

"That was cool!" Trent recalled happily. "I didn't like the river, though. I put my foot in it and my toes practically got frozen!"

"Good Lord! They took these kids to the river at night while they partied!" Rafe's eyes met Holly's. "That could've ended in a catastrophe!"

"But it didn't. The boys are right here, safe and sound."

"But the girls aren't! They got away with their little river dance and feel invincible enough to try it again." Rafe rubbed his hand over his face. "Damn, why don't I know what goes on around here?"

He was clearly distraught by the boys' revelation. Holly's heart went out to him. She dismissed their earlier argument, along with the hostility that went with it. This was no longer about her; they'd already moved on to a new crisis, one that rendered his game-playing accusation frivolous. The man was trying to do right by his four charges, but the girls, at least, seemed determined to sabotage his best efforts. A not uncommon occupational hazard in dealing with adolescents—particularly rebellious ones.

"Camryn did show some modicum of responsibility when she was baby-sitting," Holly said, trying to focus on a positive aspect. She always tried to find something praiseworthy amid the debris of troublesome behavior. "She didn't want to leave the boys home alone so she took them with her. True, her judgment was, um, skewed but—"

"Okay, okay, okay!" As if conjured up by their conversation, Camryn's voice, loud and annoyed, suddenly boomed through the telephone receiver. "I'm here!"

The volume of music in the car was so high that the four in

the kitchen could've danced to it, had they been so inclined. None of them was.

"Bring my car back right now, Camryn," Rafe commanded.

"What if I don't?" the girl challenged.

"Then I—I'll call the police and tell them to arrest you for car theft. That's grand larceny, Camryn, so don't push me. You won't like prison one bit."

"Me, in jail!" exclaimed Camryn gleefully. "In the slammer. The cooler. The pen."

"The big house!" a male voice in the background chimed in, and there was a chorus of raucous laughter, both girls' and boys'.

Rafe's lips tightened. Naturally she'd collected her cadre of antisocial pals. "You have a half hour to get the car back here, Camryn. Or I swear, I'm calling the cops."

There was more laughter from within the car. "Do what you have to do, half bro, 'cause I won't be back in half an hour," Camryn said sassily. "'Bye!"

She hung up, leaving Rafe clutching the receiver, his dark eyes snapping with sheer unadulterated rage. He redialed, and the ringing began anew.

"How come you didn't ask her where she was going?" Trent asked as he and Tony trotted to the freezer for more Popsicles. They returned to their perches on the counters, resigned to more waiting.

"Out of the mouths of babes," Holly murmured.

Rafe shot her a look. "She hung up before I could ask," he muttered.

Holly propped one shoulder against the wall, surveying the scene. "Making unrealistic threats has been unequivocally proven to be ineffectual," she remarked casually.

Rafe glowered at her. "Exactly what do you mean by that?"

"Just that you aren't going to call the police and report your car stolen so—"

"Oh, no? Just watch me!" Rafe began to punch in another series of numbers.

"When an underage teenager takes the family car without permission, it's certainly irritating, maybe even maddening, but it is not car theft," said Holly. "The police know it, you know it, and Camryn and Kaylin and their friends know it, too."

Rafe replaced the receiver in its cradle with such exaggerated care that Holly knew he was restraining himself from slamming it down.

"Spoken like an expert on legal statutes," he said caustically. "Are you a lawyer as well as a shrink?"

"Rafe's a lawyer," Trent piped up, watching the two adults with interest.

"Which makes your grand larceny threat even less believable," Holly added.

"You are accusing me of being ineffectual?" Incensed, Rafe started toward her. He stopped directly in front of her.

But Holly did not back away. She knew instinctively that he would never physically hurt her. Anyway, she had already been this close to him—and much closer. Far from being intimidated, she had the strangest urge to put her arms around him, not in a sexual come-on, but to offer comfort and support.

"I didn't mean that *you* were ineffectual," she said, her voice quiet and calm and infinitely soothing. "You're smart, dependable, and committed to the kids and they know it. But your threat to have Camryn arrested for grand larceny car theft is...well, ineffectual."

"I bet that's the same tone you use to assure a paranoiac that the TV set isn't transmitting secret messages into electrodes implanted in his brain." Rafe grimaced wryly. He placed his hands on her shoulders, then resisted the almost overwhelming urge to pull her against him. Just to hold her. She felt so good in his arms.

"The TV set can transmit secret messages?" Trent gasped. "Cool!"

Rafe quickly dropped his hands. Not only couldn't he hold Holly, he had to watch what he said to her because they had an audience.

Holly's lips twitched. "Rafe was making a joke, Trent." Hesitantly, she laid her hand on Rafe's arm. "Do you want to use my car to go look for the girls?"

He nodded. "Let's go."

As the four of them piled into Holly's car, Rafe realized that he'd intended to use her car even before she'd made the offer. It had been a given because somehow she'd become as much a part of the search as himself and the boys.

He slanted a quick glance at her. She was sitting next to him in the front seat, half turned to show the boys in the back how to work her portable phone.

"Keep trying to get the girls," Holly instructed. "And if they answer, the first thing you want to ask is exactly where they are and where they're headed."

"If I'd done that instead of making unrealistic, ineffectual threats, we might know where the little demons are right now," Rafe said under his breath for her ears only.

"You were under stress," Holly said patiently.

"Tactful of you not to suggest better communication skills for my half sisters and me."

"The three of you could use some help in that area, Rafe. But you already know that, so I won't press the point."

"I don't want to discuss it, Holly. At least, not now," he added in grim concession to the point she wasn't pressing.

Holly nodded and turned her attention to the unfamiliar scenery whizzing by. She was getting a rather unorthodox introduction to her new hometown—and meeting her new next-door neighbors had definitely taken an unconventional turn—but she couldn't imagine things happening any other way. It all seemed oddly fated.

She glanced back at the boys who were taking turns punching in the numbers on her car phone. They found the concept of dialing once and letting it ring on and on too boring. Beside her, Rafe steered the car onto another, less crowded road while the speedometer rose. Holly pondered why being with them seemed so normal, so right. She'd only known them a few hours yet she felt strongly connected to them, as if they had been part of her life for years.

"Hey, Rafe, you know the first time Camryn took us to the river?" Trent called from the back seat. "We had pizza before we went there. It was the hugest pizza I ever saw and Grable and Becker got another one 'cause they were still hungry."

"That's a really good clue, Trent. Do you remember anything else about the pizza place?"

"There was a pool table there," Tony put in. "And a pinball machine. I played it."

"I think they're talking about DeLallo's," Rafe said to Holly. "It's mainly a bar, but families go there in the early evening because they claim to serve the biggest pizzas in the state. They probably do, too—they use these special pizza pans twice the usual size."

"Is it anywhere near the river?" Holly asked hopefully.

Rafe nodded. "Less than three blocks."

There was a wooded area bordering the banks of the river, and they cruised slowly along the road until spotting Rafe's green Grand Cherokee parked on the shoulder. An overgrown patch of tall weeds and scrub bushes and trees nearly surrounded it.

"You found them!" Holly was astounded.

The search had seemed hopeless to her. The Big Sioux was long and meandering, and there was no guarantee that the girls and their friends were actually headed to the river anyway. She knew enough about kids to figure that Camryn and Kaylin might've used a decoy destination, expecting Tony or Trent to tell Rafe, thus throwing him totally off their course.

But here was his car.

They all climbed out, and Rafe started toward the river. "I'll go first. You three follow me single file, and if I tell you to watch out for poison ivy or poison oak—watch out for it."

Holly went last, putting the children between her and Rafe. His poison ivy and oak warning already had her itching, though he didn't spot the plants. In less than two minutes they stood alongside the swiftly flowing waters of the river on a stretch of dark ground littered with rocks—and clothes.

"They went skinny-dipping!" Rafe was outraged.

"And they took off their clothes, too," added Tony, not getting the term. "This is Grable's Viking shirt. See how big it is!"

"Here's Camryn and Kaylin's clothes!" Trent ran over to a flat rock where two neat piles of girls' clothing were stacked.

"I'm going to kill them!" growled Rafe.

"Where are they?" Holly peered into the water. "If they're swimming, shouldn't we be able to see them?"

As if on cue, shouts sounded from the water, far from shore.

"Hi!" Trent and Tony hollered, jumping up and down and waving their arms. "Hi, hi! We're here!"

"They're in trouble." Rafe kicked off his moccasins.

For a split second Holly thought he meant the girls would be grounded or lose phone privileges or face some other adolescent-oriented punishment which he planned to impose. Then she realized that he meant something else entirely. Something ominous, something dangerous.

The trouble was the river. The teenagers were floundering in the water and crying for help.

"Holly, go to the car phone and call 9-1-1 for help. Tell them exactly where we are," Rafe ordered. "Trent, you and Tony go to the Jeep and get those blankets we keep in the back." He stripped off his shirt and jeans as he spoke. Wearing only a pair of gray boxer briefs, he waded into the water.

"Rafe, don't go in, wait for help to arrive!" Holly cried. "You can't rescue all of—"

"Make that call right now, Holly," he shouted over his shoulder. "And don't any of you even think of putting a toe in this water!"

He was still wading, the water only midcalf, but Holly knew that rivers were unpredictable and therefore, treacherous. The depth was often deceiving, shallow in places but with unexpected, unseen dropoffs. If he were to step into a hole, he could be in way over his head, literally. And then there were the currents, both surface and deep, to knock him off balance and drag him under.

The teenagers appeared to be experiencing some of those dangers right now.

Holly ran to the car, keeping a watchful eye on Tony and Trent. Rafe had warned them against going into the water but they were so active, so impulsive, she worried that they might race each other into the river on a dare.

She made the 9-1-1 call, pinpointing their location as best as she could. Her unfamiliarity with the area was frustrating, and she feared she wasted some valuable time because she couldn't answer the questions as specifically as needed.

Trent and Tony each carried a blanket they'd taken from the back of the Grand Cherokee as the three of them tramped back through the vegetation to the riverbank. Two, tall, muscular teenage boys had already pulled on their clothes and stood, wet and glum, staring out at the river.

"That's Grable and Becker," Tony told Holly.

"You can't have these blankets 'cause they're for the girls," Trent called to them.

Holly hurried over to the older boys, wishing she had her medical bag with her. They had been in such a rush to leave, she hadn't thought to bring it along so there wasn't much she could do for Grable and Becker except time their pulses and respirations. Which fell well within the normal range. Although serious medical consequences could result from swallowing too much water, the two teens were not experiencing any symptoms of it.

She was suddenly, intensely furious at these big stupid boys who not only had endangered themselves but also Camryn and Kaylin—and Rafe. Her heart lodged in her throat as she watched three dark heads bobbing far out in the river. Sam, the third teenage boy whose hair was a bright distinctive red in color, was paddling furiously to keep afloat.

"Camryn wanted to come here, not us." Grable appeared to be on the verge of tears. "We said we didn't want to go in the water but she made us."

"Camryn is about one-third your size. There is no way she could've forced you into the river!" Holly was exasperated. "You should have stopped her."

"Camryn does whatever she wants," whined Becker.

"Next you'll tell me the waters of the Big Sioux will part on her command!" Holly snapped. Their unabashed irresponsibility was grating on her nerves, and she found it more and more difficult to maintain even a semblance of calm. "Tony, get away from the water!" she called to the child.

Tony, who'd edged near enough to the river to wet the toe of his shoe, came running back to stand beside her. "I wasn't going in, Holly."

"You've got that right," Holly replied.

Trent, standing on the other side of her, chuckled. "Now you kind of sound like Rafe."

They all watched as Rafe dragged Kaylin toward the shore. "Stay right here and don't move," Holly ordered Trent and Tony—though Grable and Becker immediately froze in place, too. She kicked off her shoes and ran into the river to wrap the blue blanket around the sobbing Kaylin.

"We couldn't get back to shore," she cried. "And then we got tired. Camryn kept going under. Camryn!" She screamed her sister's name.

Rafe had already swum away from them, back into the water. "Rafe will get her," Holly said soothingly. She had expended her anger on the hapless Grable and Becker because she felt only compassion for Kaylin and had no urge to scold her.

"What if Camryn drowns?" Kaylin cried harder. "What'll I do without my sister?"

She was shivering and shaking so hard that Holly had to dry her off with the blanket and help her dress, all the while maintaining a watch on her vital signs. Kaylin's pulse was rapid and thready and she was gasping for air.

"Camryn is going to be all right," Holly promised, though she was normally against providing broad assurances, especially ones not based on hard facts.

Yet what else could she say to this youngster who was trembling with shock and terror? She fought the urge to deliver a homily about risk and regret. The psychiatrist within knew the timing was all wrong for a lecture. But later...

As the rescue squad came tramping through the underbrush to the riverbank, Holly recalled Dr. Widmark informing her of her appointment to the Teens At Risk Task Force here in Sioux Falls. It seemed downright karmic that two teens who were definitely at risk lived in the adjoining duplex. Later, when the threat of imminent danger was past, when the time was right for it, she was going to help these girls, Holly vowed.

And she was going to encourage Rafe to admit his connection to them, something that needed to be put into words, to be expressed and heard. Though Rafe hadn't hesitated to plunge into the river to rescue his sisters, actions weren't enough. His *half* sisters, Holly silently corrected herself because the trio seemed so hung up on the distinction. But there was nothing halfway about Rafe's commitment to Camryn and Kaylin. He'd proven that again today.

Holly spied Rafe pulling Camryn to shore and rushed into knee-deep water carrying the other blanket to wrap around the girl. The rescue team went in after Sam, a ruggedly built boy, whose predicament confirmed Holly's theory that size and strength offered no safety guarantees against the perils of a fast-flowing river.

Both Sam and Camryn seemed to be in worse shape than the others, weak, coughing and choking into the oxygen masks provided by the rescue crew. Kaylin received oxygen, too, though she remained fully alert. The team acknowledged Holly's credentials as a doctor but didn't let her treat their patients. She didn't try, staying out of the way while the paramedics performed their duties.

Kaylin pulled off her oxygen mask. "Is Camryn going to die?"

Holly put her arms around the girl. "No, but all of you will have to go to the hospital, Kaylin."

"But why? I want to go home!" Kaylin cried. "We're okay, just let us go! You can't force us to go to any stupid hospital!"

"Hospitalization is mandatory for all near-drowning victims, kid," one of the paramedics said sternly. "And put that mask back on."

"No!" Kaylin screamed. "You can't make me! We didn't drown, you can see that we're okay."

"Just ask your friend the doctor here about delayed death from hypoxia," grunted another paramedic, clearly fed up with Kaylin's hysterics. He looked at Holly. "Tell her, Dr. Casale."

Holly replaced Kaylin's oxygen mask and took her cold small hands in her own. "Consciousness isn't synonymous with recovery, Kaylin," she said quietly. "They aren't bluffing—delayed death from hypoxia can and does occur."

Kaylin's protests ceased. "W-what's hypoxia?" She mouthed the words.

"Lack of oxygen to the tissues of the body. Ingesting too much water can cause damage to the lungs and critical—fatal—changes in blood chemistry. All of you need medical attention to rule out or monitor any of those consequences, Kaylin.''

Kaylin removed the mask again. ''If Rafe hadn't come...'' She stared at her brother who stood a hundred yards away between Trent and Tony, watching the paramedics work on Camryn and Sam. ''We would've drowned for sure, huh?''

''I think that's probably true.'' Holly didn't try to sugarcoat it. There were times when a reality check was necessary despite the terror it induced. ''Your brother was terribly worried about you, Kaylin. He cares about you and your sister very much.''

''Even after this?'' Kaylin whispered. Her young face was a portrait of fear and desperation. Her eyes fastened on Camryn lying on the gurney, being carried to the ambulance. ''Flint and Eva are going to tell him to send us away.''

Holly hugged her. ''Rafe isn't going to send you and Camryn away, Kaylin.'' She knew she had no business making a promise that was only Rafe's to make. But all her instincts told her that it was true.

Holly gazed at Rafe, now talking to one of the policemen who'd arrived on the scene. She noticed that he was fully dressed. She hadn't seen when, but sometime during the ensuing commotion he had pulled his shirt and jeans back on.

Over the soaking wet boxer briefs? The totally irrelevant thought jumped into her mind—along with an image of him wearing them. It seemed that she'd stored a detailed vision of him, unclad, in a very accessible section of her brain. She saw his chest and back, bare and bronzed, his well-shaped, muscular legs. And she saw the wet cotton of his briefs conforming precisely to the most virile portion of his body. Which was very virile indeed. Giddily, she seemed to recall every descriptive slang term she'd ever heard pertaining to that crucial masculine part.

Holly was dumbfounded. She was a doctor, she never had such frivolous lustful thoughts! However, remembering the bawdiness of some of her med school classmates, she conceded that being a doctor probably had nothing to do with it. She'd simply never before looked at a man in scant attire and experienced a carnal surge.

No, it had not been the proper Dr. Casale who'd stored those enticing mind pictures in her head for later review—it was Holly the woman, who had always taken a back seat to her own compelling drive and ambition.

Suddenly, it was difficult to breathe. Holly forced herself to concentrate on Kaylin, still soaked and clinging to her. She replaced the despised oxygen mask and comforted the girl. By the time Rafe walked over to them, Holly managed to look like the consummate professional that she was. She hoped.

"They're taking Camryn and Sam to the hospital in the ambulance," said Rafe. "I'm going to follow with Trent and Tony and Grable—he's that big imbecile that I would very much like to dismember. Would you take the other one?"

"The other imbecile you would like to dismember?" Holly's lips quirked. "If it's any consolation, I felt the same way at first. It passes."

"If you say so, Doc. And will you take Kaylin with you, too? The paramedics say she doesn't require treatment en route and think she'll do better riding with you rather than them. No wonder. You managed to calm her down."

Almost absently, he took Holly's hand and carried it to his mouth, lightly touching his lips to her knuckles seemingly before realizing what he was doing. He quickly dropped her hand.

"Of course." Holly's heart was turning queer somersaults in her chest. If she'd been hooked up to an electrocardiogram machine at this moment, the readings would be very peculiar indeed.

"Can she walk to your car?" Rafe nodded toward Kaylin. He almost placed his hand on the girl's shoulder but he pulled it back, as if unsure whether to touch her or not. "Or should I carry her?"

Holly observed his uncertainty and was moved by the concern in his offer. If only he'd directed it to Kaylin herself, if only he'd given in to impulse and patted his younger sister's shoulder. Yes, the family could definitely use some help developing communication skills but she was optimistic because she'd seen their fledgling allegiance to each other. The necessary connections were there even if the Paradises didn't seem to know it themselves.

"Kaylin, do you feel up to walking?" Holly asked for Rafe.

"I think I'm going to hurl," Kaylin gasped.

She whirled out of Holly's embrace, ran a few steps, and promptly vomited. Holly held her head. As soon as the crisis passed, Rafe picked up his sister and strode toward Holly's car.

She followed with the four boys. Grable and Becker were wet, scared and subdued. Trent and Tony raced and bounced with excitement.

The ambulance and police car were leaving as Rafe deposited Kaylin in the front seat of Holly's car. Becker slumped in the back, a very damp blanket wrapped around him.

"The hospital is about twenty minutes away," Rafe said. "Follow me there."

It was a brisk authoritative command but this time Holly didn't take offense. She'd learned a lot about Rafe Paradise in the few hours she'd known him, knew she could hold her own with him. And if he needed to sound in charge to cope with the situation, she was willing to accept that.

Five

Rafe's head spun with the inscrutable terms the ER doctors were throwing around. Laryngospasm, hypoxemia, hypercapnia, and the not-to-be-dismissed, atelectasis. Fortunately, Holly was there to conduct an intelligent discussion with them because Rafe knew he couldn't have even faked it.

Dispatched to the waiting room together yet again, Holly explained that the teenagers were being treated to prevent the sinister-sounding complications and were in no imminent danger.

"Then why clobber us with gruesome details of conditions they don't even have?" Rafe demanded.

"This is a teaching hospital," Holly explained patiently. "Did you notice the group in the white coats—the ones that looked about the same age as Kaylin and Camryn—who crowded into the examining room with us? They're medical students, and the doctors on call were using this as a teaching opportunity for them."

"And you believe that family members of the patients here should be bludgeoned with horrifying medical possibilities as a teaching exercise?"

Rafe felt outrage flow through him, and it felt good. It warmed and strengthened him. He welcomed the revitalizing anger. It helped erase the sheer terror of seeing Camryn and Kaylin struggling for their lives in the river.

"I won't bother to answer that since you're looking for a fight and will argue with any explanation I give."

Rafe frowned. Too bad she was right. Worse yet, she knew it and had called him on it. Still, he couldn't seem to let up. "So you not only shrink minds, you read them, too, Doc?"

"Back to shrink-bashing?" Holly arched her brows. "You really are desperate for an argument, aren't you? Sorry, but I'm not going to give you one."

She walked to the far corner of the waiting room where Trent and Tony were attempting to shake down the snack machines. Literally.

Holly handed them some more coins, which they immediately deposited. "This place is pretty cool," Trent remarked, looking around him. "A big TV, soda, stuff to eat. If there were video games here, it would be perfect."

"Yeah!" Tony seconded enthusiastically. "But I don't wanna watch the news. Let's go change the station." They hurried over to the television set that was mounted on the wall, climbed onto chairs to reach the controls, and proceeded to channel surf.

"I know this is a teaching hospital." Rafe picked up their earlier conversation as if there'd been no interruption.

He'd come to stand beside Holly at the snack machines. Since their arrival at the hospital, he seemed unable to stay more than a foot away from her. He tried to tell himself it was because her medical knowledge and status made her invaluable in dealing with the staff but, in all honesty, he knew that was only part of it.

The other part, the main part... Rafe swallowed. He couldn't deal with that, not here, not now. "Eva is doing her internal medicine rotation at this place."

"She is?"

Rafe nodded. "U.S.D. med school teaches the first two years of its science curriculum at the campus in Vermillion and the last two years of clinical training elsewhere. This hospital is one of the ones in Sioux Falls affiliated with the program."

Holly digested this. "Are you going to call Eva and tell her that her two younger sisters are in the ER and will probably be admitted overnight for observation?"

"I probably should, but I'm not up to dealing with another episode of the family feud just now." He shrugged resignedly. "You've already heard Camryn's and Kaylin's opinions of Eva. Well, it's mutual, I'm sorry to say."

Holly recalled the comments about wicked Evita, the witch doctor. It was safe to assume that, "Eva doesn't like the girls, either?"

"Oh, you could say that." Rafe smiled grimly. "But it would be more accurate to say that Eva loathes them."

"Why is that?"

"You've met Camryn and Kaylin, Holly."

"Yes, I have, and I don't loathe them, I like them. Furthermore, you like them, too." Holly's eyes widened. "Is that why Eva loathes her long-lost sisters? Because she's jealous of—"

"You know, if I were paying you by the hour I might understand your interest and your questions," Rafe cut in sharply. "I might even appreciate it. But since that's not the case..."

His voice trailed off and he focused his eyes elsewhere. "Tony, stop jumping off the chairs! And quit messing with the color on the TV, Trent. Nobody wants to watch green people."

"So Eva is jealous because the girls are living with you," Holly murmured. "She preferred to be the one and only little sister and resents Camryn and Kaylin for usurping her position."

"Save a word like *usurping* for your head-case articles in your shrink journals, Holly. It doesn't belong in normal conversation. Just hearing it makes me want to throw something."

Holly was not the least bit threatened. "Poor Rafe. It has to be terribly disheartening. You do the right thing and take in your orphaned little sisters and then have to deal with your other sister's jealousy and anger toward them—of which you end up bearing a substantial brunt, I would guess." She stared up at him with brown eyes, earnest and warm.

Rafe gazed into her eyes. She was perceptive, he had to give her that. "The whole situation has been hard on Eva," he said quietly. "Tough for her to deal with."

This time Holly said nothing, either for or against Eva. She just kept looking at him with those beautiful eyes of hers. All of a sudden, Rafe felt like talking about things that he'd always considered off-limits in conversation.

"Our mother died of meningitis when Eva was only six and within a year, our father married a volatile, vindictive witch—except it's spelled with a 'b'—named Marcine."

"And this Marcine person is Camryn and Kaylin's mother?"

"Yeah. It all happened so fast we hardly knew what hit us. Mom died, Dad married Marcine, Camryn and Kaylin were born twelve months apart, and then Marcine split with the babies. We never saw or heard from them again. Not that we ever wanted to see Marcine again. Flint and Eva and I were thrilled she was out of our lives but losing the two little ones..."

"You might've hated Marcine but not the children."

"They were very lovable as babies," Rafe muttered uneasily.

He'd shocked himself by disclosing the turbulent Marcine chapter of Paradise family history because he never discussed it with anyone, not even Flint and Eva. *Especially* not Flint and Eva, because they all agreed that rehashing the unalterable past was a futile waste of time.

He dragged his eyes from Holly's. "You are a good listener, Doc, I have to grant you that."

"Rather grudgingly granted," she said dryly, "but thank you. Would you mind if I asked a question?"

"Probably."

Holly asked it anyway. "Why didn't you see or hear from Marcine and the children again?"

"It wasn't for lack of trying on my dad's part." Rafe was immediately on the defensive. "He tried to find them, he even hired a private investigator but Marcine kept moving from place to place. She always seemed to be one step ahead of the P.I., who probably wasn't the best in the field, but was all Dad could afford at the time. When Dad was killed in a car accident six years ago, we half expected Marcine to show up demanding money for the girls or at least a copy of the death certificate to put in a claim for social security benefits for them. But there was no word from her at all."

"She never intended the girls to be found, no matter what," Holly surmised.

"It sure looked that way. We dropped the P.I. and didn't bother to hire another one. And then out of the blue, I got a call from Marcine after fourteen years of not hearing a word from her. She said she was dying, she'd contracted some virulent form of hepatitis that had destroyed her liver. She was hoping for a transplant but felt the need to make arrangements for the girls in case things didn't work out."

"Hearing from her after all that time must have been..." Holly paused, searching for a word that wasn't judgmental or presupposing. "Strange," was her best attempt.

"Now *there's* an understatement." Rafe heaved a deep sigh. "Marcine was her same hostile self. She made sure I knew she considered me a last resort, that there was nobody else to take the kids. Her only living relative was an elderly great-aunt who was bordering on senility and would never be granted guardianship. She said how much she hated having to ask any Paradise for anything. In her mind, I was only slightly above leaving the girls in the hands of the state child-welfare bureaucrats."

"Did she get her transplant or did she have one that failed?" Holly was curious.

"She died waiting for a liver, and I went to Las Vegas to bring the girls here to live with me like I'd promised. That was a little over a year ago." He heaved a sigh. "The rest is Paradise family history—everyone hates everybody else."

"Nobody hates you, Rafe."

He didn't seem to hear her. "When I said I'd take Camryn and Kaylin, I was promising our father not Marcine. I know how much he wanted to find those kids. It seemed so unfair that when they finally came back to Sioux Falls, he wasn't around to see them."

"It is unfair," Holly said softly.

"Not that a reunion would've been easy, even if Dad had lived to see them. Camryn and Kaylin's minds have been poisoned against him by their mother all these years. They insist Dad didn't want them, that he was cruel to their mother—all lies, but they won't listen to any other version. Flint and Eva go nuts whenever those two start spouting all that garbage about Dad.''

''And Camryn and Kaylin find a way to work it into every conversation with them because they know the response they'll get. Am I right?''

''Exactly right. More mind-reading skills, Doc?''

''I don't read minds but I do have knowledge of adolescent behavior with some grief reaction research mixed in,'' Holly countered calmly. ''The girls feel they have to prove their loyalty to their dead mother by—''

''Their father is just as dead,'' Rafe cut in sharply. ''What about loyalty to him? He was the one who was truly wronged. Marcine stole his children!''

Holly knew it was time to back off. This was neither the time nor the place for an in-depth discussion of motives and behavior, though one was sorely needed by all parties involved at some point. But not now. She cleared her throat.

''Would you like me to contact Eva and tell her the girls are here? I could approach her on a professional level, one doctor to another. This is one of the hospitals where the Widmark practice has privileges, and that would include me.''

''You think Eva, a lowly med student, wouldn't dare go nuclear around an attending physician?'' Rafe tried to decide if he were offended or amused.

''It wouldn't be a wise move on her part,'' agreed Holly.

She knew from her own experience that while in ''doctor mode,'' one was trained to keep control, to hold back and refrain from impulsive emotional responses. She had mastered the role well; she couldn't remember the last time she'd lost her cool around a patient or even a colleague. Maybe way back in her early days as a med student?

Another insight suddenly struck her. She had so successfully detached her emotions in her professional life that she'd become equally reserved in her personal life. Why, she could even mask her exasperation when her family was in the throes of their marriage madness!

''I know your intentions are good, but you don't have to protect me from my own sister, Holly. I'll tell Eva myself if and when I feel the time is right.''

Rafe's voice jolted her from her reverie. Holly stared up at him. God, he was a marvelous-looking man. And every time she looked at him, he seemed sexier, more handsome—even after a harrowing dip in the river!

She swallowed. Rafe had effortlessly penetrated her facade of cool. She grew hot remembering how fast, how completely, she'd melted in his arms. How he had felt and tasted.

Holly quickly turned away from him. Her whole body was flushed and her mind faltered in a morass of confusion. These thoughts she kept having, these feelings... It was all so completely unlike her.

''Rafe! Jensen Montel told me you were here!'' A rumpled, tired-looking young woman with Rafe's distinctive bronzed features and sleek black hair came barreling into the waiting room. The starched, white, hospital-issue jacket she wore was several sizes too large for her, as if she'd grabbed someone else's coat in a rush.

''I hope you feel the time is right now,'' Holly whispered. ''Because unless I'm wildly mistaken, I bet that's Eva—and that she already knows about the girls.''

Eva did know. ''Oh, Rafe, now they've really done it! Those miserable rotten brats could've gotten you killed!'' She threw her arms around her brother and hugged him hard. ''Are you all right, Rafe? Have you been treated yet? You have to have—''

''I'm fine, Eva, I don't need any medical treatment.'' Rafe patted her back. ''But Camryn and Kaylin—''

''I know they're being taken care of. Everybody is running around catering to them!'' Eva was indignant. ''But you're the one I'm worried about—going into that river, risking your life to pull those worthless little monsters out of the water. Oh, Rafe, if anything would've happened to you—''

''Eva, honey, nothing happened to me. I was never in danger, and I don't need to be treated for anything. If you don't believe me ask—'' He looked over Eva's shoulder and his eyes met Holly's.

Taking the cue, Holly stepped forward. ''I'm Dr. Holly Casale. I've recently joined the Widmark family practice," she said in her calm, measured physician's voice.

The effect on Eva was instantaneous. The younger woman quickly straightened and moved out of her brother's embrace. She held out a trembling hand to Holly. "Pleased to meet you, Dr. Casale. I'm Eva Paradise. I—I'm in my internal medicine rotation, assigned to Dr. Gordon."

Holly gave a brief nod, as if she knew exactly who Dr. Gordon was and how he fit into the hospital hierarchy. She assured Eva that her brother had not been harmed by his sojourn in the river and then, because just last year she'd been a senior resident in charge of med students, she quizzed Eva on the symptoms of acute reflex laryngospasm in near-drowning victims.

Eva coughed, as if she were suffering from it herself. "I—haven't had my ER rotation yet," she murmured.

"Laryngospasm is covered in anatomy class." Holly frowned. She expected better of women medical students because they were judged more strictly by both their peers and their superiors. "Maybe we ought to review the physiology of the larynx..." She gazed expectantly at Eva.

Eva gulped.

"Oh, for crying out loud, knock it off," Rafe snapped at Holly.

"Rafe." An aghast Eva grated her teeth. "Please! Dr. Casale is right, I should know this. I *do* know it."

She started to recite the physiology of the larynx at the same moment that a nursing assistant marched out to order Trent and Tony to leave the television alone. The two boys made a beeline to Rafe's side.

"Oh, no!" Eva was clearly appalled by their presence. "*They're* here, too?" She glanced vexedly from the boys to Rafe.

"Can we go swimming now?" asked Tony. "You promised, Rafe!"

"*Swimming!* Rafe could've drowned in the river today rescuing those two bratty idiots and now you want him to go swimming with you?" Eva was not pleased. "Where? Back in the river? Oh, well, why not? Camryn and Kaylin are currently out of commission but you two are still around to pick up the slack!"

"Hey, Evita, I'm gonna tell Camryn and Kaylin you said they

were bratty idiots," Trent retorted. "And anyway, we saw Rafe in the river and he didn't almost get drownded. He ruled the water, man!"

"Dr. Paradise, I suggest that you study the charts of the three patients who are to be admitted for overnight observation for possible symptoms of hypoxia." Holly used the icy tone she reserved for unprepared med students on the psych service back in Michigan. "That will include your two younger sisters, of course. And spend some time this evening reviewing everything you should already know about the anatomy and physiology of the larynx, and the repercussions of aspiration."

It was a tone guaranteed to send intimidated young med students running to complete the assignment and had the intended effect on Eva. She gave Rafe a quick hug, murmured a deferential goodbye to Holly, then hurried off.

"Wow! You sure got rid of her fast!" Trent was impressed.

"Now can we go swimming?" pleaded Tony. "Not in the river," he added hastily, "in the motel pool."

"That sounds like a good idea," said Holly. "I'll find a motel with a pool off I-90." She turned to Rafe. "How about if I take the boys while you stay here with your sisters? I'll call and let you know where we are, and you can pick up Trent and Tony tonight when hospital visiting hours are over."

A mixture of relief, gratitude, and reluctance flowed through Rafe. He knew Trent and Tony couldn't stay in the waiting room much longer without dismantling it. If Holly hadn't offered to take them, he would've had to call the Steens—no, he couldn't call them because they were at the Great Plains Zoo... He raked his hand through his hair. There was nobody he could've called, certainly not the boys' mother who would've whined and wept while making excuses for her unavailability. Holly was a godsend.

But he didn't want her to leave. He was sure that things would go a lot easier for him, Camryn and Kaylin here at the hospital if she was with them. And what if Eva decided to make another appearance? He didn't have to imagine the fierce scene that might erupt between the sisters; he'd lived through enough of them already.

Abruptly, he felt guiltily disloyal to Eva. Holly had treated her like a lowly marine recruit in the presence of the all-powerful drill instructor, and he hadn't done anything to stop it. He really should have interfered. Eva would probably spend half the night studying the damn larynx, expecting to be grilled on the material the next day.

Poor Eva, she'd looked so tired and had been so scared for him. He knew how much his little sister loved him. They'd always been close, and he had been her anchor since their father's death when she was only nineteen. Who could blame her for resenting the others who had staked their own claim on him?

Holly Casale could. And clearly did.

A streak of resentment surged through him. What was happening to him? He'd always been steady and solid—Flint had nick-named him Reliable Rafe, the Family Rock—but with Holly, he was different. His emotions kept bouncing from one extreme to another. Around her, he was more flake than rock.

Common sense dictated the most obvious solution to the problem would be to avoid her. And he intended to, Rafe decided, as he watched her walk through the doors of the ER with Tony and Trent. Later.

Holly had bypassed the motel chains and found a small family-run place called the Great Plains Motel on a highway just off the interstate exchange. It boasted a pool, a coffee shop and a gift shop loaded with a spectacular collection of gimcrack souvenirs. Trent and Tony had loved it all.

They'd played in the pool for hours. Many of their water games revolved around a drowning-and-rescue theme that Holly found fascinating from a psych point of view. She knew that children used play to work through their fears, and despite their sanguine attitude at the time, it seemed Trent and Tony had been quite anxious when Rafe and the girls had been in the river.

From a personal point of view, she'd enjoyed the boys' enthusiasm for everything. They were fun to have around. After swimming they'd eaten dinner in the coffee shop and she treated them to their items of choice from the gift shop.

Trent wanted a rubber tomahawk. "I'm part Lakota Sioux, like

Rafe,'' he'd informed her, while Tony fell in love with the most repulsive rattlesnake replica Holly had ever seen.

She'd found their antics amusing and would've liked to share them with Rafe but when he arrived to pick up Trent and Tony, he was distracted and brusque, interested only in herding the kids into his Jeep and leaving. Worse, he tried to reimburse her for what she'd spent on the boys' snacks, dinner and souvenirs.

Holly had refused his money and after they'd gone, she wondered why she felt so insulted by Rafe's offer. After all, some people would've been incensed if he hadn't made it. The children weren't her financial responsibility. She had fulfilled the role of good neighbor simply by baby-sitting.

She had no right or reason to feel either hurt or anger at the cool distance Rafe had maintained with her. It wasn't as if he'd blown her off. He was tired, concerned about his sisters, preoccupied...

He'd blown her off!

Holly faced the truth. Wasn't she always encouraging patients to face reality rather than hide from it? She certainly ought to practice what she preached.

She took a long shower and washed her hair, pulling on a new nightshirt, a lighthearted goodbye gift from her friend Brenna. It was a one-size-fits-all shirt with Looney Tunes characters in pajamas imprinted on the front. Holly gazed down at herself. The one-size fit her like an awning. She would have to remember to tell Brenna that a gorilla as big as King Kong could easily wear this nightshirt.

The phone rang, startling her. She reached for it, her heart suddenly thundering in her ears.

A familiar voice sounded, and her racing pulses instantly decelerated. ''Hi, Mom.''

A few hours ago she'd left a brief message on her parents' answering machine, letting them know she had arrived safely in Sioux Falls and where she was staying. She had added she was simply reporting in and that they needn't return her call.

''I know you must be feeling so lonely there, stuck in a motel room, your furniture lost on that truck. It's probably halfway to

Wyoming right now and you won't see it for weeks," her mother lamented. "So I called to cheer you up."

"I'm fine, Mom. But it's good to hear your voice."

Her mother filled her in on the latest wedding news. Little Heidi had been positively glowing at the bridal shower thrown for her by one of Aunt Honoria's closest friends. "We all missed you, Holly. How I wish you could've been here for it."

"Mmm." Holly stared at the paint-by-numbers picture of two Siamese cats hanging on the wall. They looked vaguely demonic, their eyes a startlingly vivid blue.

"I was so sure you'd end up marrying Devlin Brennan, Holly," her mother said wistfully.

Holly tuned back into the conversation. "Mom—"

"You were so close to Devlin all through medical school and when you both accepted residencies at the hospital in Ann Arbor, I was absolutely positive that you two would get married." Helene sighed with audible regret.

"Mom, Dev and I were always just good friends," Holly cut in. "I told you that for years. I don't know why you wouldn't believe me."

"Just friends!" Her mother sniffed. "That's what movie stars say when they're hiding a torrid affair. Everybody knows that."

"Mom, Dev and I aren't movie stars, and there was no torrid affair to hide."

"Obviously. Devlin married another woman and they have a child." Holly could almost see her mother's shoulders slump in disappointment. "I still can't believe it, Holly. All those times he came home with you, all the time he spent with us whenever we visited you in Ann Arbor—and then he went and married someone else!"

Holly didn't bother to explain that she'd brought along Devlin Brennan to deflect the blind dates she knew would otherwise await her. Dev's presence was pure camouflage, despite her repeated claims of friendship only. She was fully aware those claims would be misinterpreted; she'd counted on it. Holly knew the family mindset well. If there was a man at her side, there would be no lengthy inquisition and/or harangues about "boyfriends." Or the lack thereof. Dev had been a great sport to go along with her, though he'd never pretended to be anything other than her friend when they were alone.

Because that's all she had ever been to him. His pal, his buddy and study partner, and one of his best friends. Devlin Brennan had never guessed that Holly was in love with him, and she had certainly not told him. He was now happily married and a devoted father, and she'd actually had a hand in making it all happen. Not that she would dare break that news to her mother!

Thinking of Dev brought memories of the easy camaraderie their longtime friendship had provided. She'd never known another man she felt so comfortable, so very herself with. Involuntarily, the image of Rafe Paradise flashed to mind.

She was uneasy and edgy with him, which was not surprising. How could she feel comfortably chummy with Rafe after experiencing those stunning flashes of physical attraction, the fierce, strong surges of desire?

Holly tried to recall having similarly intense sexual feelings for Dev and couldn't. But she must have early on, when she'd first decided that she loved him. Hadn't she?

If so, she no longer remembered. And whenever she thought of Devlin Brennan now, it was always with a kind of bittersweet tenderness, a warm understanding and acceptance of who and what he was. They had shared so much during those crucial years training to be doctors, and now he was Gillian's husband and baby Ashley's father. Holly knew he loved them deeply. He was happy, and she was glad for her dear friend.

Her mother wasn't. "You wasted years of your life on Devlin Brennan," mourned Helene. "And now you're far away in Sioux Falls where there aren't any available single men and—"

"There are available single men here in Sioux Falls, Mom." Another image of Rafe Paradise appeared before Holly's mind's eye before she firmly erased it. No, she was *not* going down that road!

"But will you ever meet any of them? You need to get out more, Holly. Both Ann Landers and Dear Abby recommend taking an adult education class—one of interest to men, of course, something to do with cars is good—or working on a political campaign as a way to meet a mate."

"I'm not interested in taking a car class or working on a political campaign, Mom."

"Well, I've heard that Parents Without Partners is an excellent place to meet somebody."

"I'm sure it is—for parents. I'm not a parent, Mom," Holly reminded her.

Her mother pointed out that she never would be one if she didn't do something about her woeful marital status. And soon! Her biological clock was ticking so loudly they could hear it back in Michigan. Et cetera, et cetera. Holly began to unpack her suitcase while her mother continued to bemoan her solitary life.

"The invitations to little Heidi's wedding go out this week. Of course, you'll be coming home for the wedding, won't you, Holly? You've always been Heidi's favorite cousin and Aunt Honoria is arranging something special for you." Helene Casale provided a grand finale to wrap up the conversation. "She knows a wonderful man who can't wait to be introduced to you and he is going to be invited to the wedding..."

Merely imagining the latest matrimonial candidate to be sprung on her gave Holly a chill. Would it be completely awful if she were to boycott the wedding? She would do it tactfully, of course, invent a fictitious emergency, a life-and-death situation involving a vulnerable patient whom she simply couldn't leave for any reason.

An hour later Holly was half watching a broadcast of headline news and half concocting a plausible tale to free her from attending little Heidi's wedding, when a knock sounded on the motel room door.

And another knock, followed by a voice. Rafe's voice. "Let me in, Holly. I know you're not asleep, I can hear the television."

Holly sat up straight. She couldn't let him in, she didn't have a robe to put on over her nightshirt. Of course, she could tell him to wait while she got dressed but Holly rebelled at that tactic because she could almost hear her mother and her aunts and her sister and her cousins advising her to do just that. To doll herself up in something fetching. And to put on makeup and do something with her hair which hung in a wild tangle of damp curls.

Holly glanced down at the huge cotton nightshirt which covered more skin than any of her summer clothes. The hem hung several inches below her knees and the square-cut sleeves billowed around her elbows. She didn't really need a robe; the white cotton was so thick as to be opaque.

No, she didn't have to worry about being alluring in this getup. Not that she wanted Rafe Paradise to find her alluring, Holly reminded herself. She didn't!

"Open the door, Holly," Rafe commanded through it.

She opened it, just a crack. After all, his presence here could be due to an emergency. "Has something happened at the hospital?"

"No, I called a half hour ago, and the girls are fine." Rafe pushed open the door and walked inside the room. "Are you mad at me?"

"Why should I be?" She was pleased to hear how calm she sounded. Not rising to the bait, giving away nothing. A clinician in tone and attitude.

Rafe closed the door behind him. "I blew you off earlier," he said bluntly.

Holly was a little surprised they were of one mind on that. But she had no intention of agreeing with him because it elevated everything to a different level, one she wasn't ready to deal with. "No, you didn't."

"What would you call it then?" he challenged.

"Perfectly understandable. You were exhausted, Trent and Tony were clamoring for your attention, you've had a long, incredibly difficult day." Holly shrugged. "I didn't take anything personally, I certainly didn't expect you to—"

"I blew you off and you took it personally," Rafe cut in. "When I was leaving, you shot me a look that could freeze fire." When she opened her mouth to protest, he held up his hand to silence her. "Oh, yeah, I saw that look. It was definitely personal. You expected..." He paused. "Something better than what I gave you. I'm sorry, Holly."

"You didn't have to come the whole way over here to tell me that, Rafe." Holly took pity on him. He looked miserable, tired and tense and guilty. There were so many demands on him, and he took them all very seriously.

"Didn't I?"

She saw he was studying her, his dark eyes intently focused. "I bet you didn't know that Yosemite Sam slept with a nightcap over his cowboy hat," she said jokingly about one of the cartoon characters on her nightshirt, the one she thought he was staring at.

Except when she glanced down, she noticed Yosemite Sam was positioned directly on her left breast—and that her raised nipple was prominent against the cloth.

Holly took a step backward. "Where are the boys?" Her voice was husky and breathless, as far from her proper clinical tone as could be.

"The Steen kids were waiting for them when we got home. They wanted to camp out in their backyard tonight. Curt and Margie—the parents—had a tent all set up with sleeping bags and flashlights and snacks. How could I say no to that?"

"How indeed?" His smile made her heart rate double. No, triple. "The Steens sound nice."

"Yeah. You'll meet them tomorrow. They want to welcome you to the neighborhood." He rubbed his neck with his hand, then rolled his shoulders in an effort to alleviate the muscular tension.

Holly watched him. "Feeling the effects of your rescue mission?"

"I feel like I've gone a few rounds in a barroom brawl." Rafe laughed slightly. His other hand moved to his lower back and he winced. "I never realized how many different muscles could be sore and stiff at the same time."

"You were using all of them swimming against the current and dragging the girls into shore. The Big Sioux River is a mightier opponent than any you'd find in a bar. Are you all right?" Holly asked softly.

"Sure. I'm fine."

"Would you admit it if you weren't?"

He shook his head. "Of course not."

"I didn't think so. Men are terrible patients. They either go the macho stoic route or agonize over any little ache."

Rafe's smile widened. "Actually, you sound a lot like Eva.

She's already had her share of run-ins with the crybabies and the stoics.''

"Tell her it'll only get worse." Holly looked at him. "I have some ibuprofen and muscle relaxants in my bag. I'll give you some to take at home."

"Forget the muscle relaxants." Rafe recoiled as if she'd offered him heroin. "The ibuprofen, I'll accept. And a massage." He sat down on the bed. "They teach you how to do that in medical school, don't they, Doc?"

Holly handed him the tablets and a glass of water, trying to ignore the sudden meltdown occurring inside her. He was only kidding, wasn't he?

After swallowing the ibuprofen, Rafe pulled off his blue and white cotton shirt, exposing an expanse of sinuous, coppery chest. Holly's breath caught in her throat. Apparently, he wasn't kidding.

"Should I lie down?"

His voice held a distinct note of...of *something* but Holly's usually fail-safe powers of perception seemed to have shut down, and she couldn't divine exactly what. Daring? Teasing? Seduction?

He didn't wait for her assent and lay across the bed on his stomach, angled sideways to accommodate his long length. His back was as smooth and muscled and bronze as his chest. Holly tried hard not to gape. His body was beautiful, at least the part she could see.

Her eyes flicked over the length of his well-worn jeans. He wore them well, all right; his behind, his long, long legs were a true work of masculine art. She vividly remembered how he'd looked getting out of the river, his soaked boxer briefs clinging intimately to his male form.

Rafe raised himself slightly on his elbows and turned his head to look at her.

"Forget how to do it?"

Again, that note in his voice. Holly decided it was all three: daring, teasing, and seductive. And she wasn't sure how to respond. "Of course not."

"You sentenced Eva to a night of studying the old anatomy

text. Maybe you ought to do the same, huh, Doc? Review the muscles of the human—''

"I was a straight-A student in anatomy class and I haven't forgotten a single muscle, nerve, or bone," Holly retorted, silently scolding herself.

She was behaving like a schoolgirl instead of a doctor who'd seen more male bodies than she cared to count—including many completely nude ones. Of course, those bodies had belonged to patients in the hospital, and she hadn't been remotely attracted to any of them.

Holly attempted to steady herself. If she stopped to compare how completely different this situation was, she might make a total fool of herself. A massage. That's all he had asked for. All she had to do was to give him one.

She was a doctor, governed by her brain not her hormones. Her self-control had been legendary during her years at Michigan; she'd never let foolish impulses divert her.

A massage. She could do it. There didn't have to be anything more to it than that.

Six

Holly climbed onto the bed to kneel next to him. Starting at his neck, she slowly began to work her fingers over the tense, knotted muscles. A low groan escaped from his throat. Due to the painful tension in those sore muscles? Holly caught her lip between her teeth and massaged on, working her way down to his shoulders.

It quickly became obvious that she couldn't reach both his shoulders kneeling beside him like this. Nervously, she climbed onto him to straddle his hips, trying to ignore the feel of denim against her bare inner thighs. As she leaned forward, her nightshirt rode up a little, but it was such a tent she had plenty of room to maneuver within it.

Holly worked her hands down one side of his back and then the other, her fingers diligently massaging, increasing the pressure enough to unlock the stiff muscles. Next she concentrated on his spine, her thumbs revolving around each vertebra.

Her movements caused her hips to rock against his. Heat blazed through her like rocket fire and hit every erogenous zone in her body, including her head. It was suddenly imperative to say something, anything, to break the sultry silence that seemed to have displaced the air in the room.

"I—probably should be using lotion. A professional masseuse usually does. But I, uh, don't have any lotion with me, just some facial cream I use at night. I guess I could use that but it...it—" She was aware she was starting to babble, and her face flushed with embarrassment.

Be quiet and concentrate on the diagrams of the muscular system we had to memorize back in anatomy class, Holly commanded herself. *Recite the name and function of each muscle as you work.*

A worthy diversion, except it wasn't working. The feel of Rafe's hard back and smooth skin under her hands was undermining her resolve in a major way. The sensations evoked by sitting on him, her legs apart, were beginning to render her mindless, hardly surprising as it was a provocative position on a bed in a quiet motel room.

Forget being rendered mindless, she was already there, Holly admitted dizzily. She'd lost it the moment she had talked herself into giving this massage.

She smoothed her palms down the length of his back, her weight pressing him deeper into the mattress. "I have to stop now." Her voice sounded heavy. "My arms are getting tired."

Which was true, but beside the point. She felt hotter than she'd ever felt in her life and knew if she didn't get up, if she didn't get away from him... Holly shifted and moved off him to kneel beside him. She couldn't seem to move any farther.

"What about my pectorals?" Rafe's voice sounded muffled and faraway as he named the muscles that connect the chest with the bones of the upper arms and shoulders. "They're really sore after all that swimming and dragging the girls through the water."

Rafe kept his eyes closed, but the tension gripping his body had nothing to do with the exertion of the river rescue. He couldn't remember ever being so turned on. The touch of her hands on his bare skin had transported him to a zone of sensual rapture. And feeling her straddle him, her bottom bouncing up and down as she massaged him with those talented hands of hers, was close to erotica nirvana.

"I—I really think—" Holly's voice caught in her throat when he suddenly rolled over, revealing his very obvious condition.

She felt a momentary relief that his eyes were closed because she couldn't help but gawk at the significant bulge in his jeans. He was obviously, visibly aroused.

Rafe opened his eyes and caught her staring at him, her eyes agog. "Come here," he said huskily.

Holly saw the hunger in his gaze, the same desire that she knew burned in her own. She ought to back off now, to stop this before it went any further. She'd been deluding herself that physical contact between them could begin and end with a massage.

Rafe reached out to run his hand along her forearm, then his fingers fastened around her wrist, manacling her. "Let's finish what we started, Holly." He tugged her gently.

Of course, he could be talking about the massage. She could pretend that was what she thought he meant. But Holly didn't bother with any more rationalizations as she allowed him to pull her closer.

Their gazes locked; she slowly brought her hips to rest over his. She felt his clothed erection pressing hard against her, and they both gasped at the contact.

Holly laid her hands on his chest and slid her palms up to his shoulders. She massaged them silently, watching in fascination as her fingers played over his muscles.

Rafe lay quietly, barely breathing. She didn't know if his eyes were open or closed, she didn't look to see. She was mesmerized by the actions of her hands on his body.

Boldly, her fingers trailed down to his stomach and traced the deep, concentric shape of his navel. Rafe drew in a sharp breath and she smiled at his reflexive response. It encouraged her, emboldened her to do more, to touch him in ways that had nothing at all to do with a therapeutic massage. She traced his nipples with her fingertips, teasing the taut buds as her own ached and tingled vicariously.

Rafe watched her through slitted eyes. What she was doing felt so wonderful he didn't want her to stop, yet he could no longer remain the passive recipient of her caresses. He had to touch her, to see her. Always a man of action, he had to take charge.

He slipped his hands under her voluminous nightshirt and stroked her legs, gliding his palms up and down the backs and exterior sides of her thighs a few times before moving to the smooth and satiny interior skin. Holly remained locked in place, unable to move or speak or do anything at all as his big hands slowly inched along her inner thighs, his fingers kneading and caressing a path of fire all the way to the juncture between her legs.

He traced the outline of her bikini panties before cupping her bottom. Holly's heart seemed to stop completely, then lurch to a pounding start as he brought his thumbs together between her thighs. He pressed and stroked the sensitive area, and Holly moaned. Her thought processes, already overwhelmed, boomeranged between ecstasy and embarrassment. Her panties were wet and now he knew it. He knew how aroused she was, how much she loved what he was doing to her, how much she wanted him. When he withdrew his hands, she whimpered a protest.

"It's all right, baby, I just want to get you out of this thing," Rafe said, his voice soothing. He whipped off her nightshirt and she lifted her arms to assist, complying automatically before his words had even fully registered in her mind.

For a few charged moments both were still, Rafe lying on his back, Holly astride him wearing only her white cotton panties. She felt his eyes devouring her, lingering on her breasts, her belly, her legs.

"You are so beautiful," he whispered.

He lifted his hands to cup her breasts, fondling their rounded softness, lightly squeezing and shaping before brushing her tight pink nipples with the tips of his fingers.

Holly watched him, the sight so erotic that she couldn't tear her eyes away. Rafe continued to play with her breasts, his caresses unhurried yet intent. She moaned helplessly, caught in a sensual trance induced by the exquisite, unfamiliar pleasure.

She had never given any man access to her body like this, had never ceded control of herself to anyone.

Rafe moved his hands to her waist, over the concave flatness of her stomach. His fingers were careful, as if she were delicate and needed special handling.

Maybe she did.

"You're tense." His voice surrounded her. "Don't be nervous, Holly."

"I don't want to be." She swallowed hard. "But I—I don't do this all that much." Her shaky circumlocution embarrassed her; she sounded like an inarticulate kid.

"Do you want to stop?" Rafe asked quietly.

Her body, newly awakened and aroused, nearly rioted at the notion. Holly gazed into Rafe's eyes. They were almost completely black, the pupils dilated with desire, eyes that were fiery with passion and desire. He wanted her, she could see it in his gaze, feel it in the rigid male hardness throbbing against her. But he would accede to her wishes. If she said stop, he would. She knew it.

Paralyzed by indecision, Holly made no reply. She didn't trust her own judgment when it came to sex, not after her first and only disastrous experience when she was just sixteen. She had been among a group of high school kids back then, their minds blotted from too much beer and their hormones running high one Friday night in an empty suburban house.

That night she'd given in to sexual curiosity and entered a bedroom with one of the older boys whose high school credentials were impeccable, an athlete with good grades who was popular with the right crowd. When they began kissing, she imagined the two of them becoming the newest couple in school, she pictured them going to the prom together.

Unfortunately, what she had learned that night was that sex was a painful, humiliating mess, and a fumbling drunken tryst resulted in neither a boyfriend nor a prom date. It didn't even rate a follow-up phone call. Her first lover, if that term could be applied to him, never acknowledged her existence again, not even to say hello when they passed in the halls at school.

A traumatized Holly had tried to put it behind her by dropping out of the partying crowd and concentrating on her studies. Her grades soared, earning her all kinds of academic awards. She remained equally focused during her college and med school years. In her psych residency, she'd put her adolescent pain and anger

to good use, easily accessing it to connect to the troubled teenagers who needed her understanding counsel.

"You look like a scared little girl." Rafe sat up, holding her
on his lap. Her thighs were on either side of his, her hands on
his chest. "You don't have to be afraid of me, Holly. Don't be
afraid."

The calming resonance of his voice had a hypnotizing effect
on her. Holly lay against him, her eyes closing. He brushed her
hair from her neck, then began to kiss the tender skin, nibbling
and nuzzling while his hands moved leisurely up and down her
bare back. She gasped and arched into him when he found a
particularly sensitive spot just below her ear. He nipped at the
skin, then sucked it, pressing her tightly to him.

Her breasts were crushed against the warm strength of his
chest, her nipples throbbed so fiercely the pleasure bordered on
pain. She could feel him hard and insistent between her legs, and
he rocked against her, making her burn for him, making her ache.
She wanted him so much, needed him so much she thought she
was going to die if he didn't, if they didn't...

The wildness that rushed through her abruptly, paradoxically
restored her control. Holly stiffened, once again assailed by memories of that other night in another bedroom so long ago. She'd
been a girl, excited and nervous and impulsive, blindly throwing
away caution and common sense with a boy she didn't know very
well, a boy who had made no commitment to her or even offered
any words of love.

Flash forward to the present. *The more things change, the more
they stay the same.* Where had she first heard that adage? From
TV, a book, her mother? She couldn't recall, but the sentiment
certainly rang true.

Now she was a woman who was behaving like an excited,
nervous, and impulsive teen. She was on the verge of throwing
away caution and common sense with a man she'd known less
than a day. A man who had made no commitment to her nor
offered any words of love.

Not that she would've believed him if he had. She was neither
gullible nor naive. They hardly knew each other; the possibility
of caring and commitment were out of the question. There was

just sex—and though it promised the pleasure and thrills losing her virginity had lacked—Holly knew she shouldn't go through with it.

"Rafe, I can't do this," she said breathlessly. "Please, I—I'm sorry." She tried to move off his lap but he held her tight, restraining her.

Even as her pulses leaped in alarm, Holly recognized that some would say she deserved whatever she got for letting things go this far. If she didn't want to have sex, she had certainly sent out all the wrong signals, and now, now...

Rafe released her, lifting her off his lap and setting her beside him on the bed. He grabbed for his shirt and pulled it on. "You were right. Coming here was a bad idea."

Holly fumbled for her nightshirt, which had been turned inside out when he'd yanked it off. At the moment she didn't possess the dexterity to remedy it, so she pulled it on, the seams on the outside, the cartoon decals rough against her skin.

She rose to her knees on the bed. "That's not what I said, Rafe. Not what I meant."

Now that he was walking toward the door, she felt bereft, anticipating the long sleepless night ahead and already missing him. "Oh, no!" she groaned, shaking her head back and forth. "I sound like one of those insipid twits I either pity or make fun of. Oh, Lord, I—I've turned into one!"

Rafe stopped and turned around. "Insipid twits?" His lips twitched.

"You know, women who give out so many mixed signals that a man needs an unscrambler to comprehend what they mean." She stared glumly at the ugly industrial gray carpet. "I didn't realize till now that it isn't intentional on their part, that the women themselves don't know what they mean."

"You're anything but an insipid twit, Holly."

"Thank you." She raised her head and met his eyes. "You're a true gentleman, Rafe."

"No, I'm not." He reached into the pockets of his jeans and pulled out four foil packets. "I fully intended to go to bed with you tonight. I came prepared for it."

Holly's eyes widened and she stood up. "*Four* condoms? You...you can do it *four* times in a night?"

"Well, hope springs eternal. And I live by that old Indian motto, Be Prepared."

"I thought that was the Boy Scout motto."

Rafe shrugged. "Whatever." He moved closer to her and pressed the foil packets into her right hand. "I'll leave these with you for safekeeping. And no, that's not a bad pun."

Her fingers closed around the unexpected gift. It occurred to her that she had never owned any condoms. Given her celibate life-style, there had not been any need for them. "Rafe, I—I think I can explain what happened between us tonight."

"Mind if I quote Camryn and Kaylin? 'Duh!' What's to explain, Holly?"

"I mean, scientifically. Psychologically." Holly swallowed, determined to make some sense of her wildly-out-of-character behavior, if only for her own peace of mind. "There have been well-documented studies about the effects of strong emotions on physical arousal, especially when danger is involved. The girls' near-drowning in the river this afternoon certainly qualifies as dangerous."

Rafe folded his arms and eyed her archly. "You do have a tendency to overthink everything, don't you?"

"Physical arousal is manifested by symptoms like heart palpitations, nervous tremors, flushing and accelerated breathing." Holly plowed on, quoting one article from memory. She'd always found it easy to retain what she studied and to apply the material to given situations. "When a person experiences these symptoms, all that remains is to identify them as passion, and if a man and woman are together when in this condition, they—"

"Forget the psycho-babble," Rafe cut in. "We were hot for each other before we went anywhere near the river." Two giant steps put him right back within touching range. "So much for your adrenaline-makes-the-heart-grow-fonder theory, Doc."

Holly reached out to touch him. She couldn't stop herself. Her palms spread over his chest and she tilted her head to gaze up into his onyx eyes.

He rested his hands lightly on her hips. "Do you want me to

stay, Holly?'' Rafe lowered his head, and lightly nuzzled her nose with his.

His lips brushed hers in a soft, almost chaste kiss, but the banked fires of sensuality were so powerful that heat surged through her. Holly closed her eyes, shuddering with delicious pleasure. Lying to him was not an option.

''Yes,'' she whispered.

Her tongue feathered against his lips, and he groaned and pulled her tighter. His sound of need pierced the very core of her, liquefying her resistance and heightening her own need. When Rafe took her mouth, his tongue plunging deep within, Holly sagged against him, clinging to him, responding hotly to the possessive kiss.

She wrapped both arms around him, bringing herself even closer, wanting more. Deep inside, she was aching and empty and yearning for something she'd yet to know. But she wanted to know it and to experience it with Rafe. Only him.

His hand closed over her breast, plucking at the nipple, and a bolt of sensual electricity zinged from the pebble-hard tip to deep within her womb. Holly uttered a sharp, shocked cry, both alarmed and tempted by what he was making her feel and how much she wanted it—and so much more.

Rafe lifted his head. ''You're killing me here, Holly.'' His voice was deep, almost guttural. One hand remained on her breast, the other kneaded her bottom. ''You have to tell me now. Are we going to bed or should I go home?''

Holly wanted him to stay so much that a sudden rush of emotional tears filled her eyes. She licked her moist, swollen lips with the tip of her tongue.

Abruptly, Rafe released her and stepped back. ''I need that unscrambler you mentioned earlier. You look like you're going to cry.'' The possibility clearly unnerved him.

''Rafe, I—I think it's only fair to explain that I— Well, I do have some...some unresolved issues pertaining to sex.'' She watched him retreat a few steps.

If the sight of her tears had shaken him, listening to her intellectualize sent him heading straight for the door.

''You're not ready for this, Holly.'' He opened the door. ''And you're probably right, we are going way too fast. You need time, we both need more time. After all, we'll be living next door to each other. That's going to be tough enough for you without throwing sex into the mix.''

He stepped outside, pausing to call over his shoulder. "Good night and thanks for all your help today.''

That last remark of his sounded a lot like the president of a service club addressing volunteers at the end of a successful fund-raiser. Holly sank onto the bed and clutched her head in her hands. Rafe was an experienced adult male and behaved like one, whereas she'd been confused and unsure. It was as if she'd been frozen sexually in time to her sixteen-year-old self, the girl so filled with shame and regret about the miserable night she'd lost her virginity that she had avoided sex from then on for her own self-protection.

Her perspective shifted drastically, suddenly revealing her behavior since then from a totally different angle. There was her universal rejection of all those potential mates dredged up by her family, her dogged belief that she was in love with Devlin Brennan who had never even attempted to kiss her. Because she hadn't sent out a single subtle signal that she would welcome his advances—or anyone else's?

Until she'd met Rafe Paradise, she had been as sexually comatose as Sleeping Beauty or Snow White before being kissed awake and alive by the handsome, desirable prince. Holly stretched out on the bed, reliving the feel of Rafe's hands and mouth, of his hard body next to hers.

She wanted him desperately, but she had undoubtedly alienated him forever. Bad enough she'd said no after her responses gave him every reason to believe she meant yes. She had made the situation even worse by attempting to explain things in a pedantic way guaranteed to send any normal man running. Especially one who had known her less than twenty-four hours. Rafe had enough going on in his life; the last thing he needed was to listen to her own bungling self-analysis!

Holly picked up the four foil packets that had dropped to the floor when she'd become too caught up in kissing Rafe to remember to hold on to them. He had arrived at her door looking to make love—hopefully four times!—and she had treated him to a full-blown episode of sexual angst and uncertainty.

I do have some unresolved issues pertaining to sex. Aaargh! She'd actually said that to him! Holly cringed, blushing.

She switched off the lamp and the television set and crawled into bed. It was going to be awkward seeing Rafe again, though she knew she would have to. Their next-door neighbor status guaranteed it. She tried to ignore the sticky heat between her legs and the dull throbbing in her lower abdomen, tangible symptoms of her very real desire for him.

How was she ever going to face him tomorrow?

Yet unnerving as the prospect was, she couldn't wait.

Just when he thought that no day could possibly be worse than yesterday, today dawned.

Rafe pulled the Jeep Grand Cherokee into his driveway, and Camryn and Kaylin climbed out and stormed into the house. They had been discharged from the hospital and he'd brought them home this morning, informing them on the way that they were indefinitely grounded for taking his car without permission, not to mention that death-defying dip in the river.

Neither girl took the news well. Rafe had half expected the pair to be chastened or scared by yesterday's near disaster, but they were as defiant and argumentative as ever. Maybe even worse, because Kaylin was usually more agreeable than Camryn, but today she was equally quarrelsome.

Rafe sat behind the steering wheel, the engine turned off, seeking a temporary reprieve from entering the house and resuming hostilities. This morning's clash with his half sisters wasn't even his first sibling skirmish of the day.

Earlier, Eva had apprehended him in the hospital corridor on his way to collect Camryn and Kaylin from their room.

"When are you going to stop playing the martyr and ship those nasty little brats back to Nevada where they belong, Rafe?" Eva launched her offensive without preamble. "Sending them to you was Marcine's ultimate revenge. They belong with that relative of hers, not here with us."

"I already told you that I met Marcine's great-aunt. The poor old soul is pushing ninety, Eva. Most of the time she thinks F.D.R. is president and worries about rationing and who'll win World War II. She could no more cope with Camryn and Kaylin than she could surf the World Wide Web.''

"So the alternative is to let them ruin your life?" Eva demanded bitterly.

"My life is not ruined, Eva." Rafe tried to be patient.

"Rafe, you don't have to pretend with me. I love you and I worry about you. I know your life is intolerable. All you do is work and go home to the trouble and chaos those kids are always causing. And that includes Trent and Tony, too. Their hapless airhead of a mother has foisted them on you, and it's just not fair! You're being mercilessly taken advantage of and it has to stop. *You* have to stop it!"

Rafe didn't try to explain or argue with her. What was the point? Eva considered him either a long-suffering martyr or a masochistic chump. Rafe knew he wasn't, but her misperceptions rankled, and so did the fact that his own twin shared Eva's opinion of him.

Flint had made that clear again last night.

His brother had been waiting for him at home when he'd arrived after his botched attempt to make love to Holly Casale. Rafe had been in no mood to see anyone after that debacle, not even his identical twin.

He'd spent last night's drive from the motel back to the duplex grimly debating whether Holly had a major sexual hang-up or was a manipulative tease or was simply wiser and more controlled than he by halting an impulsive one-night stand.

Not that he was into one-night stands himself. He wasn't, and he instinctively knew that one night with Holly Casale would never be enough, though admittedly, he had neglected to mention that crucial fact to her.

His whole body ached with urgency and need yet his passion for her was stronger than ever. He was as *ambivalent*—yes, he was familiar with that term so beloved by her profession—about their relationship, or lack thereof, as she was. Not a good sign at all.

But his plans to take an ice-cold shower and bore himself to sleep by watching infomercials on late-night television were shattered by Flint's unexpected presence.

"Eva called," Flint said, explaining his impromptu visit. "She told me all about the Demonic Duo's latest antics. After all the rain we've had this summer, the Big Sioux River is running fast and high and you could've drowned going in after those brats, Rafe. It's a miracle that you—" Flint stopped himself. "No, not a miracle. That old saw about the devil protecting his own definitely applies here. That's why Camryn and Kaylin didn't drown before you got there."

"You're saying I was covered by some sort of blanket immunity for rescuing the spawn of Satan?" Rafe attempted to joke.

"Exactly." Flint wasn't kidding. "Rafe, those kids—"

"They're our half sisters, Flint. They're Dad's daughters."

"They're Marcine's daughters, Rafe. She took them away from Dad and erased any influence or effect he might've ever had on them. If he were here—"

"They would be living with him, Flint. Dad never stopped thinking about them, you know that. He left them those shares in the company and—"

"For god's sake, don't ever tell them they own a piece of Paradise Outdoors!" Flint exclaimed. "I can just imagine those mercenary little wretches hooking up with some sleazy lawyer to sue for their shares, disrupting the business, causing even more trouble than they already—"

"I'm the girls' legal guardian and I have no intention of telling them that they own a quarter of the family company between them," Rafe assured his twin. "I know they're too young to handle it, that money is for college and—"

"College? Those two birdbrains?" jeered Flint. "I've never met two less likely candidates for college in my life. You're living a pipe dream if you think any college will take them, brother. Or is that, smoking a pipe dream? Or smoking some other kind of—"

"I get your point, you don't have to drive it into the ground." Rafe sighed. "Kaylin's grades aren't good, I agree, but she has the ability to do better. And Camryn is smart, Flint. Really smart. Her English teacher told me Camryn was one of the best writers she's had in fifteen years of teaching. I saw some of her essays—marked with things like 'Perfect. Nothing to correct' and 'Outstandingly creative' and 'A brilliant piece of writing.'"

"Well, if Camryn is so brilliant and creative, how come the little rat flunked English and had to go to summer school to make up the course?" demanded Flint.

"She didn't fail because she was stupid. Camryn had a bad habit of only showing up for class and turning in assignments when she felt like it, and threats of flunking didn't motivate her to conform. Still, the teacher hated to fail her though we both agreed it had to be done. Interestingly enough, she pulled an A in the course this summer because she did all the work. The teacher and I got together and planned a combined—"

"See, that's what really bothers me, Rafe," Flint cut in, staring at his brother with concern. "Why should you have to traipse to school every other day to placate outraged teachers? You deserve to have fun, you should be carefree, not trapped by this faux family you're stuck with. Your life has been derailed by those kids, and that includes Trent and Tony, who belong with their mother. The boys are *her* responsibility, not yours."

"My life hasn't been derailed, Flint," countered Rafe. Somehow hearing his brother say what he himself often thought compelled him to disagree.

"You had an active social life before your house was invaded, Rafe. But when was the last time you had a date? The last time you had sex?"

"I could ask you the same questions, brother."

"True, but they wouldn't apply. I'm a workaholic. My life is running Paradise Outdoors, and I like it that way. You're the sociable one, that's why you were always the popular twin, not me." Flint laughed, mocking the frequent attempts to consign twins to disparate slots though he and Rafe actually were personality opposites. "I'm the quiet twin, remember? You're the friendly one everybody likes."

"Ever think that *I* worry about you and Eva and *your* lack of a social life?" Rafe decided that sometimes the best defense was a good offense, and not only in football. "You say that being president of Paradise Outdoors is enough for you, and Eva says that her hours at the hospital and studying for her classes take up all her time, but maybe you two are using your work as an excuse to hide.''

"To hide from what?" demanded Flint.

"From dating, from the opposite sex.'' His brother looked so indignant, Rafe knew he'd hit a nerve. "Maybe you're wary of women because of Dad's bad luck with Marcine, and Eva is wary of men because—'' He frowned, temporarily stuck. "Because of Dad's bad luck with Marcine.''

So what if he was being repetitive? Marcine was a veritable gold mine of pathology.

"That's the biggest crock I've ever heard!" Flint spluttered. "Did you read an article in *Psychology Today* at the dentist's office or something?''

No, but he'd spent the day in the company of a psychiatrist. Maybe some of Holly's ability to analyze had rubbed off.

Inspired, Rafe continued. "You've taken Paradise Outdoors from a small niche company and broadened the customer base to a national scale. As a lawyer I respect your business savvy, as part owner of the business I'm certainly appreciative of the higher income, but as your brother I'm concerned about you, Flint. You've become something of a recluse over the years, you're a prisoner of your routine at Paradise Outdoors. Your life is all work and no time for anything or anyone else. Whatever else might be said about *my* life, it isn't reclusive or routine.''

"No, it's insane.'' Flint scowled. "And so is this conversation.'' He glanced at his watch. "It's getting late and we're talking in circles. I should go.''

An unearthly howl sounded and continued, growing louder and louder.

"Hot Dog,'' murmured Rafe. "If the Lamberts were still living next door, the phone would be ringing off the hook by now.'' He grimaced at the memory of all those infuriated complaints from the fed-up Lamberts. How long would it take Holly to reach the same state?

"I forgot to mention that overstuffed werewolf masquerading as a dog attacked me when I came in,'' mumbled Flint. "Luckily,

I had my handy Paradise Dog Repellent Whistle with me. I wouldn't come here without it. It worked like a charm.''

"Naturally. All the equipment sold by Paradise Outdoors works. It's top quality and we stand behind our products, money back guaranteed." Rafe spouted the company philosophy while looking around the downstairs. "Where is that dog? He was in desperate straits earlier because we'd been gone for hours, and he couldn't go outside. He was so glad to see the boys and me he forgot to growl at us."

"The miserable beast ran upstairs after I blew the whistle. With any luck, he threw himself out a window." Flint added a quick, disgruntled goodbye and left.

Rafe had gone upstairs to find Hot Dog sitting on Camryn's bed in the room the two sisters shared. The dog had sat up expectantly, realized it was only Rafe, not one of the girls, and flopped back down with a canine sound of disappointment.

"Believe me, pal, I feel as lousy as you do," Rafe had muttered.

It was the first time since Hot Dog had invaded his home and his life that Rafe had felt any bond at all with the hound from hell. "It's been that kind of a day, hasn't it, boy?" he added in an effort to expand the solidarity.

Hot Dog just snarled.

Seven

He couldn't put it off any longer. It was time to go inside.

Rafe climbed out of the Grand Cherokee and trudged toward his side of the duplex. Camryn and Kaylin had probably spent their first fifteen minutes home from the hospital plotting their next escape. Now he had to shift into full big-brother mode and proceed with his dastardly plan to wreck his half sisters' lives. That had been Kaylin's impassioned accusation while stomping inside.

Before he reached the front door, Flint's champagne-colored Saturn pulled alongside the curb. Rafe stared, astonished as Flint and two blondes emerged from the car and headed toward him.

He recognized one of the women. She was Lorna Larson, whom he'd met on the plane what seemed to be a lifetime ago, but was actually only early yesterday morning. The other woman was taller with paler, longer hair than Lorna's.

Flint had a defiant yet triumphant expression on his face, and Rafe realized that this was his brother's retaliation for describing him as reclusive and routine. He *really* must've struck a nerve last night!

"So you actually do exist!" Lorna exclaimed, smiling vivaciously from Rafe to Flint.

Flint smiled back. Rafe looked baffled. He almost uttered a confused, "Huh?" but caught himself in time.

"I was having breakfast this morning in the Radisson coffee shop when Flint walked in." Lorna apparently realized an explanation was in order. "Of course, I thought he was you, Rafe. When he told me he was your twin, frankly, I didn't believe him."

"She thought she was being played for a fool in the old 'I'm not me, I'm my twin' scam," Flint added glibly.

"Oh." Rafe was deadpan. "That old scam."

"We started talking," Lorna chattered on, "and realized that we're both dedicated workaholics but felt it wouldn't hurt to take a little time off on a beautiful Saturday like this one."

Rafe remembered Lorna slipping him her card yesterday; this morning she'd hooked up with his brother. The woman was dedicated, but was it to work?

He watched as Lorna linked hands with Flint, who stiffened only slightly. Flint had never been physically affectionate, and holding hands with the tactile Lorna would've normally gone against his grain. Rafe realized just how determined his brother really was to continue this farce.

"Lorna still wasn't convinced I was me, even after I showed her my driver's license." Flint picked up the narrative, his face set in staunch resolution.

Rafe envisioned the scene of Flint attempting to be playful and showing the coquettishly skeptical Lorna his driver's license. He grimaced. His brother made a better workaholic than flirt.

"Well, now you know, he is Flint and I am Rafe."

"And I'm Nicolette Kline," the other blonde spoke up. "I'm very glad to meet you, Rafe, although I feel like I'm seeing double." She giggled. "Double the pleasure, double the fun."

Her recitation of the old chewing gum commercial made both brothers wince. They'd been plagued by similar riffs their entire lives.

"Nicolette works in the Sioux Falls' branch office of Lorna's company,'' Flint said, his smile firmly fixed in place. ''I thought the four of us could spend some time together today.''

Rafe barely managed to stifle a groan. Beyond a doubt, Flint had taken his comments last night as both a rebuke and a challenge and decided to prove him wrong. So he'd not only found himself a woman for the day, but also found one for Rafe.

The prospect of double dating with his twin was appalling. It was something they hadn't done since high school, and rarely even then. Worse, this was a *blind* date since Nicolette was clearly meant for him! Flint knew his feelings about blind dates—they were to be avoided at all costs—because he felt the same way about them.

Suddenly the prospect of going inside to argue away the day with Camryn and Kaylin struck Rafe as infinitely appealing. And then, while his fevered brain attempted to conjure up an excuse to escape the double date, one appeared in the flesh.

Actually three, living, breathing excuses appeared.

Trent and Tony came bounding into the front yard with Holly sauntering after them. For the first time Rafe noticed her car parked on the street along the opposite side of the duplex. He hadn't seen it from the driveway.

His eyes burned into her. She was wearing a simple lime green sundress and her hair was caught up in a high, curly ponytail. Compared to her, the blondes in their designer sports outfits looked overly dressed, overly made-up and moussed. Neither appealed to him.

But a mere glimpse of Holly caused his heart to thunder like a herd of buffalo across the plains.

''We saw Holly when we were out playing earlier and we took her over to meet the Steens!'' Tony exclaimed. ''Mrs. Steen is making her a cake and she said we can have some. It's chocolate with chocolate icing, my favorite.''

''How come you're here, Flint?'' demanded Trent, looking none too pleased. With a deepening frown, he eyed the two blond women. ''Who are they?''

''Friends of Flint,'' Rafe explained.

Holly arrived and stood slightly apart from the group. Rafe went to her side.

"They stopped by to ask me to go with them today, but I was about to tell them I can't because—" he took a deep breath, gazing into Holly's eyes, silently willing her to go along with him. "We've already made plans to spend the day together. Haven't we—" he cleared his throat "—sweetheart?"

"Yes, we're taking the children to the zoo." To his great relief, Holly didn't miss a beat. "Darling," she added drolly.

"Cool!" Trent was smiling again.

"We've been wanting to go to the zoo since yesterday!" Tony was ecstatic.

The expressions on the faces of Flint, Lorna, and Nicolette ranged from stunned surprise to mild embarrassment to annoyance.

"Why don't you two go inside and tell the girls to get ready because we'll all be leaving for the zoo soon," Holly said to the children.

"Camryn and Kaylin are coming with us?" Trent asked incredulously.

"They certainly are," said Holly.

The boys raced inside, practically tripping over each other in an effort to break the news first. Screams of outrage emanated from the house within moments.

"The zoo?" Camryn fairly flew out the door. "You actually expect *me* to—" She stopped dead in her tracks, a cartoonlike screeching halt. "Oh, yuck! It's the Evil Twin himself with Blonde and Blonder."

"Camryn!" Rafe and Flint chorused together, sounding and looking exactly alike. Disapproving and exasperated.

"They wanted Rafe to go with them but he's taking *us* to the zoo." Tony was back on the scene, glowering at Flint and the two blondes.

Kaylin and Trent joined them. "Oooh, you were right," Kaylin announced, staring at Flint, Lorna and Nicolette. She whispered something in Trent's ear and the pair broke into raucous, impudent laughter.

Rafe and Holly exchanged glances.

"Maybe this would be a good time to make some introductions?" Holly suggested gamely.

"Don't bother." Camryn was disdainful. "Why should we introduce ourselves? I don't want to know them and I certainly don't want them knowing us."

"Flint Paradise, you should be ashamed of yourself! Bringing hookers to your own twin brother's house where small children live," Kaylin scolded, draping a protective arm around Tony's shoulders. She was the picture of moral indignation.

"Hookers?" Flint blanched at the word.

"You thought we wouldn't notice?" Camryn gave a world-weary laugh. "Honestly, it's so obvious. Their hair, their clothes... What's the going rate on the street these days, girls?"

Lorna and Nicolette looked murderous but expectant, glancing from the teenagers to the twin brothers, clearly waiting for some type of disciplinary intervention.

It was slow in coming. Rafe jammed his hands into the pockets of his khaki trousers and stared silently, grimly, into space. An apoplectic Flint finally managed to speak. "Rafe, those insolent little vipers are being rude and insulting. Do something. Say something!"

Rafe heaved a sigh. This was not going well at all, and to make matters worse, he didn't particularly care that the kids had insulted his near blind date and her cohort. He sensed the kids knew it, too. Still, Flint was right, he ought to say something.

"They work in the field of telecommunications, kids."

"Oh, is *that* what they call it these days?" Kaylin sneered, and tossed her long dark hair.

Rafe caught Holly's eye and shook his head.

"I think you'd better take us back to the hotel immediately, Flint," Lorna said coldly.

"Back to the hotel for a threesome?" Camryn snickered. "What'll that cost you, Flint?"

"That's enough out of you, you miserable little monster!" His face flushed, Flint started toward her.

Camryn ducked behind Rafe and Holly. "Help! Don't let him near me! I just got out of the hospital!"

Holly felt a perverse desire to laugh but restrained herself. The irrepressible Camryn didn't need that kind of encouragement.

"Let's go inside while they say their goodbyes." She took Camryn by the arm.

"Did you see the fiendish look on my *half* brother's face? If Rafe wasn't here, he would've scalped me for sure!" Camryn called dramatically as Holly led her to the house. Kaylin and the boys followed single file, like a parade of ducklings.

"Scalping is too good for you, Camryn," Flint yelled. "You are a—"

"Flint, don't get into swapping insults with her," Rafe interrupted. "You're the adult, she's just a kid."

"I don't think she's a kid at all," Lorna snapped. "She's a bad imitation of one."

"And we do not intend to waste our valuable downtime playing nanny to a pack of insufferable brats," proclaimed Nicolette. "Flint, we want to leave right now." She and Lorna beat a hasty haughty retreat to Flint's car.

The brothers faced each other. "You can see why I don't date anymore," Rafe said wryly. "The kids feel threatened. They think if I get involved with a woman she'll convince me to kick them out. The last few times I tried to go out—well, let's just say that Blonde and Blonder got off very lightly compared to my unfortunate dates."

He surprised himself with his own insight—and by how obvious it all was. How had he missed putting it together before? Maybe Holly the Headshrinker's analytic skills really were contagious.

"Well, they seem to have accepted *sweetheart.*" Flint was watching him, his eyes narrowed. "Who is she, Rafe? You didn't mention you were seeing anyone."

"Because I'm not." Rafe shrugged. That was sort of true. Seeing each other didn't quite cover what he and Holly were doing. He didn't know what did. "But to answer your question, her name is Holly Casale and we're...friends."

Which they were, in a way. They could talk together like friends. They'd helped each other out like friends. But the sexual attraction burning between them, the desire, ruled out a simple platonic friendship.

"Friends?" Flint wasn't buying it at all. "Friends, ha! She

called you darling, you called her sweetheart. I've never heard
you call any woman sweetheart. And I saw the way you two were
looking at each other—you were practically eating each other up
with your eyes!''

''We were?''

The sharp, impatient blast of the car horn cut their conversation
short. ''You're in for one helluva day, Flint,'' Rafe observed, not
unsympathetically. ''Maybe you'd rather join us at the zoo?''

''I'd rather be eaten alive by grizzlies. As soon as I drop those
two off at the hotel—and that will be *very* soon—I'm heading
straight for the office,'' Flint muttered.

Rafe went inside the duplex to find Holly on her knees in the
kitchen petting Hot Dog. The dog gazed adoringly at her, rolling
onto his back to expose his enormous belly. As Rafe came closer,
the beast leaped to its feet and gave a menacing growl.

''Don't worry, Hot Dog, it's Rafe not the Evil Twin,'' soothed
Trent.

Hot Dog growled at the boy, too.

''Look, just cut out this Evil Twin nonsense,'' ordered Rafe.
''Flint is not evil. You all deliberately provoked him into losing
his temper. Again.''

''Flint hates us,'' Kaylin replied succinctly. ''And we don't
like him or his hooker friends, either.''

''How typical that Flint has to pay for it.'' Camryn laughed.
''He is so uncool. It's unbelievable that he's your twin, Rafe.''

''I am as uncool as he is, Camryn,'' Rafe assured her. ''And
those women weren't hookers, remember?''

''Whatever.'' Camryn's dark eyes gleamed. ''We're here and
they're gone.''

Which seemed to prove the theory he'd just espoused to Flint.
Rafe pondered his newfound psychological talents as he watched
Holly feed Hot Dog a dog biscuit shaped like a mailman. Flint
had brought up an interesting point, though. The kids accepted
Holly, and that must mean they did not perceive her as a threat.
Would they, if they knew how his blood heated by simply looking
at her?

From this angle, standing above her, he could see a small gap
in the bodice of her sundress revealing a shadowy hint of cleav-

age. He remembered the soft firm feel of her breasts in his hands last night, how she had moaned with pleasure when he touched her.

The hunger hit him with physical force. His skin felt hot and tight, and he silently cursed as he felt the swift hard response of his body to her nearness. He was lucky his trousers were loose, lucky none of the kids was looking at him. Their collective attention was focused on the dog.

He set out to break the spell the lovely lady doctor had unwittingly cast upon him. "By the way, thanks for backing up my zoo story, Holly. I owe you one," he added flippantly.

"Then I'll collect now." Holly chose another biscuit for Hot Dog, one shaped like a meter reader, which he gulped greedily. "I called the moving company this morning. The truck won't be arriving today so I really would like to go to the zoo. I don't feel like sitting around watching TV in the Great Plains Motel all day even if they do have cable with seventy-five stations."

The request was surprisingly easy to make. She had been worried that things would be difficult and tense between her and Rafe after last night's encounter, but it hadn't worked out that way. Instead they'd immediately slipped into an easy camaraderie, as if that confusing, embarrassing episode in the motel had never occurred.

She gave Hot Dog a final pat and stood up. Rafe moved at once to assist her to her feet. The feel of his hands on her triggered the sensory memories she'd been trying to suppress.

Denial was futile. She remembered every moment of their intimate interlude. It had been passionate and exciting and pleasurable beyond her wildest dreams.

Holly looked up at him. His lambent dark eyes had a visceral effect on her. Heat spread through her belly, melting into her thighs. His sensual power over her was thrilling, it was terrifying.

And they were in a room surrounded by volatile kids and a temperamental dog! In sheer self-defense, she quickly stepped away from him.

"It...will be awfully crowded if all six of us are crammed into one car." Her voice was unsteady, and Rafe smiled at the sound of it. Holly caught her lower lip between her teeth. He *knew* the effect he had on her... How could he not?

She took a deep breath and tried again. "So why don't we take two cars? Camryn, Kaylin and I could go in my car and you can take the boys in yours."

"Males in one car, females in the other? That's blatant segregation of the sexes, Holly," Rafe taunted.

"I didn't mean it to be," Holly interjected quickly. "Naturally, we can—"

"Could I drive your car, Holly?" Kaylin cut in. "I have my permit."

Holly nodded her acquiescence at once.

Rafe and his half sisters gaped at her.

"You mean, you'll really let me drive your car?" Kaylin was almost comically amazed.

Holly guessed the girl had made her request with the intention of sparking an argument and no real hope of receiving permission to drive. Now that her wish had been granted, Kaylin was flummoxed.

So was Rafe. "Are you *sure?* You don't have to let her. They've already broken a window and a TV set of yours..."

"If the state of South Dakota has issued her a learner's permit, she is legally permitted to drive accompanied by a licensed driver, right? And if she doesn't practice, how will she ever become an experienced driver?" Holly asked reasonably.

"Well, that is true," Camryn agreed. "But driving with Kaylin is way too nerve-racking." She shuddered. "I'm riding with Rafe and the boys because as much as I hate the zoo I want to get there alive and in one piece."

Kaylin pelted her with a dog biscuit shaped like a car. Hot Dog quickly snapped it up.

"You don't really have to go through with this, you know," Rafe said to Holly as they walked outside.

The four kids had already gone ahead of them and were waiting in separate cars, Camryn and the boys in the Grand Cherokee and Kaylin behind the wheel of Holly's Chevy Cavalier.

"Do you mean letting Kaylin drive or going to the zoo?" Holly asked lightly.

"Either. Both."

Their arms swung at their sides as they walked. It would've been so easy, so natural for him to take her hand in his. Rafe was a hairbreadth away from reaching for her when Holly folded her arms in front of her chest.

Another lost moment, another missed opportunity. Rafe heaved a regretful sigh.

Holly totally misinterpreted it. "I don't mind taking them all to the zoo if you'd rather do something else," she assured him.

"Like what? Chase down Flint for a double date with that pair of man-eaters?"

"First hookers, now man-eaters. The Paradise family is a tough crowd. Poor..." Holly paused. "Whoever they were. I never did get their names."

"As Camryn so bluntly put it, you don't want to know them or want them to know you."

"Is that the way you feel toward them, too?" She felt terribly petty that his disdain for the pair pleased her so much.

"Absolutely. Lorna and Nicolette—those are the girls' names—were too eager."

"Too eager?" Now she was undeniably egging him on. Holly scolded herself.

"Yeah. It's like the old Sioux legend about the wolf preferring the chase to sitting prey."

"That is an old Sioux legend? It sounds like it was lifted straight from *The Rules*," Holly muttered, suddenly irritable. Maybe she ought to offer Lorna and Nicolette her extra copies.

Because she'd seen the predatory way the blondes had been eyeing Rafe and his brother, at least until the kids appeared. And though she was not the jealous type, she'd definitely felt a nasty twinge of...well, jealousy.

She felt it now, merely contemplating the thought of other women offering themselves to Rafe. She wondered how many times in the past such overtures had been accepted by him.

Instantly her mind supplied a vivid image of Rafe lying on the motel bed last night. Holly blinked, but the image of him, masculine and virile, half dressed and aroused, remained. The way he'd touched her, kissed her...he was no novice in the bedroom, he was experienced.

Unlike her. Once again Holly felt inadequate and uptight, and she hated the turn her thoughts had taken.

She squared her shoulders. Enough of this. "They are women, not girls," she informed him. She was on solid ground there. "A *girl* is under eighteen. Certainly no older."

Rafe smiled sardonically. "I'll try not to err again. Now will you admit that you didn't like those two *women* either?"

"I don't know them," Holly replied primly. "How could I possibly say if I liked them or not? Perhaps if I knew them better, I would like them."

"Very equitable of you, Doc. Or maybe you're just plain desperate for new friends? Hopefully, not that desperate, though."

"I'm not desperate but I want to make new friends here. There's nothing wrong with that." Holly was defensive. Defiant. Determined not to yield no matter how stupid the argument. She silently conceded that this argument was stupid, indeed. "I'm new in the city and I plan to have a full social life."

"Do you?" Now he sounded as edgy as she did.

Because he was. Rafe gazed down at her. He had no doubts that her plans for a full social life here in Sioux Falls would be easily, swiftly achieved. A woman as beautiful, sweet, funny and smart as Holly would attract a host of friends of both sexes. And she was welcome to all the female pals she could fit into her busy schedule.

As for men...*that* was an entirely different matter.

A possessive streak he'd been previously unaware of surfaced, fierce and strong. Holly would be sought after by the most eligible bachelors in town, he was certain of that. In fact, Dr. Widmark's son, Collin, was considered *extremely* eligible by the Sioux Falls Junior Women's Club who had chosen him, along with a dozen others, for the Dream Date Auction, their charity fund-raiser last year. The Paradise brothers had also been asked to participate, but both Flint and Rafe had turned down that dubious honor, preferring to mail in a generous check instead of donating their bodies for charity.

Dr. Widmark was Holly's boss! Suppose he'd imported her as

a matrimonial prospect for the peripatetic Collin? Rafe's gut clenched. It seemed entirely possible—even probable. Everybody in Sioux Falls knew that the elder Widmarks were dying for grandchildren, and who better than beautiful, brainy Holly as a mother for them? As a wife for their eligible son.

Rafe, once considered a top marriageable prospect himself, knew very well that he could not be counted among that number. Not anymore. Not with a houseful of kids who could be perfectly awful at times.

Holly had already experienced some of those times during their short acquaintance. What woman would want to saddle herself with him and the responsibilities he'd assumed? Especially a woman like Holly, who had so much going for her.

Why would she? Why should she?

They stood behind the Grand Cherokee, a tense silence enshrouding them. Kaylin broke it by sounding Holly's car horn. The tribe in the Jeep countered with a blast of their own.

"Be careful driving with Kaylin," Rafe muttered, scowling at both cars. "She tends to hit the brakes hard enough to deploy the air bags."

"New drivers don't bother me. I was the only one in the family brave enough to ride with my cousin Heidi for months after she got her license."

Holly reached up to catch the curly tip of her ponytail between her fingers, a purely nervous gesture. The way Rafe was staring at her rattled her. The taut intensity on his face bordered on hostile. Or was it something else entirely? She swallowed.

The horns sounded again in earsplitting cacophony. The neighbors would not be pleased if this kept up, not even the ultra-tolerant Steens. "Tell Kaylin to follow me to the zoo," Rafe said briskly, walking to the driver's side of the Jeep.

Holly hurried to her car. A hair-raising ride with an inexperienced driver was exactly the sort of shock treatment she needed to jolt her back into being the ever-reasonable and wise Dr. Casale, who was never jealous or insecure or foolish.

It couldn't happen soon enough for Holly, who'd just proven she was all three.

* * *

"What did you do this weekend, dear?" Helene Casale asked, sounding hopeful. She always sounded hopeful, every Sunday evening during Holly's weekly phone call home.

"Yesterday I took the kids next door shopping for school supplies, Mom," Holly replied brightly. "They start back to school the day after tomorrow. Then we had dinner at the new Thai restaurant that just opened in town. Today we went to a movie and roasted hot dogs in the backyard. I just got home a little over an hour ago."

It had been a busy fun-filled weekend, but she knew her list of activities wasn't going to please her mother.

It didn't. "So you spent the *whole weekend* with those neighbors?"

"Pretty much, Mom."

"Again?" The hope was completely gone from Helene's voice. A blend of exasperation and impatience replaced it. "Holly, you've spent every weekend with them since you arrived in Sioux Falls almost a month ago. And from what you've said, you see a lot of them during the week, too. Honestly, dear, it's wonderful that you are being such a good neighbor, but don't you think it's time you went out? And I don't mean to the zoo or the museum or the mall or the movies with the family next door!"

"I'm going to a Labor Day barbecue tomorrow, Mom. The Steens, the family up the street, are having it. I'm bringing your potato salad. You know how everybody always raves about your recipe. I'm chopping the potatoes right now."

The compliment did not revive Helene's flagging spirits. "You spend too much time in that neighborhood of yours, Holly. It's nice that everybody is so—neighborly—there but really, darling, you have to get out and meet some nice *single* men."

Holly almost nicked her finger with the knife. She'd never gotten around to mentioning to her mother that there was a single man living right next door to her. Her mother assumed that the family next door, with whom she spent so much of her time, was headed by a set of married parents. Holly went along with the pretext. It was so much easier that way.

After all, it wasn't as if she and Rafe Paradise were dating or anything like that. He hadn't even tried to kiss her since her first night in Sioux Falls at the Great Plains Motel. She and Rafe were *friends,* but she really didn't want to try to explain that to her mother. Mom had never comprehended her friendship with Devlin Brennan—"But Holly, it's a waste of time for an unmarried woman to be just friends with an unmarried man"—and would be gravely disappointed to hear about yet another one.

Except this friendship with Rafe was very different from her relationship with Dev. Little shivers tingled along Holly's spine. How could she ever explain it to her mother when she didn't really understand it herself?

Comfortable as she was in Rafe's company, an intriguing subtle tension existed between them, a kind of excitement that elevated even the most mundane activities into something memorable. She was constantly aware of him, in a way she'd never been with Dev. She would've flunked out of medical school if she had been as intensely conscious of every move, every smile, frown, gesture and mood of Devlin Brennan's, but that's how it was with Rafe. How she was with Rafe.

And when she wasn't with Rafe, she thought of him. She relived things that had happened and invented scenes that hadn't. Quite a few of those fantasies were based on that one torrid evening in the Great Plains Motel. In her head, Holly didn't stop him. She imagined her body beneath his, she imagined opening herself to him, taking him deep, deep inside her.

How would it feel? She wanted to know. She wanted to know what it was like to make love with Rafe Paradise.

"Ouch!" This time Holly did nick her finger. "Oh, no, I'm bleeding all over the potatoes!"

"Be sure to wash them well before you put them in the salad, dear," her mother cautioned.

"I will, Mom. Um, tell me about Heidi's wedding plans. I hope everything is going smoothly."

"Well, there have been a few snafus. But Honoria is coping. The big day isn't far off now! I can't wait to see you, Holly. We're all looking forward to having you back with us."

Holly felt an acute pang of guilt. She'd arranged with her colleagues in the Widmark practice not to be on call that weekend, so theoretically, she could attend the wedding. But she still hadn't made up her mind to go. She had her cover story prepared—an emergency involving a fictitious suicidal patient with an abandonment complex whom she simply couldn't leave.

Suddenly the wall shook with a series of thuds. "Mom, someone's at the door."

Holly told the small white lie; it was simpler than explaining that the neighbor kids were pounding on her wall. "Can I call you back later?"

She wasn't sure if the boys were playing a round of Hit-the-Wall Ball or summoning her with an SOS. They'd tried to teach her the difference but it all sounded like cannonballs crashing to her.

"Go answer your door, Holly. I can hear the noise over the line, it's loud enough to wake the dead. And you don't have to call me back. We'll talk next week."

Holly headed next door and rang the doorbell. Camryn appeared seconds later, wearing ripped jeans shorts and an eye-popping aqua nylon halter. She held a baseball bat in hand.

"Thank God you came!" Camryn exclaimed. "I never pay attention to that Morse code stuff and I didn't know how to make an SOS. So I hit the wall with the bat and hoped you'd figure something was up."

Holly was caught off guard. Throwing balls at the wall had become routine to her, but hitting it with a bat? "What's wrong, Camryn?" she asked, concerned.

Camryn grabbed Holly's wrist and pulled her inside. "Rafe is on the phone with Tracey Krider, Trent and Tony's mother. He's up in his room and I listened in on the extension in the kitchen. There's big trouble comin' down, Holly."

"What kind of trouble?"

"Tracey told Rafe she's thinking of kicking out her psychopath boyfriend and taking her kids back to live with her. Rafe went legal-eagle on her and started yammering about custody and court and all that crap. Tracey started crying. I feel sorry for her," Camryn added, staring at Holly, her dark eyes piercing. "The boys love their mom, you know. They miss her a lot even if they don't always say so."

"Yes, I know. Almost all children love their mothers deeply, no matter what."

"You haven't met Tracey, but I have. She's not a bad person, Holly, just really screwed up. She had Trent when she was only sixteen, and she's into that whole you're-not-a-real-woman-without-a-man garbage. Puke-o-rama! She loves her kids, but she's made some stupid choices on account of her rotten boyfriends."

"You've given the situation some serious thought," Holly said quietly. "Do the boys know what Rafe and their mother are talking about?"

"No. They don't even know she's on the phone. I told Kaylin to keep them out of the way. They're in our room, playing their stupid CDs. Hear it?"

The blare of the novelty tune "Monster Mash" emanated from upstairs. Camryn looked pained. "The one before that was 'Purple People Eater'. I can't believe Trent blew his allowance on that junk!"

Holly thought of some of Camryn's CDs that she'd heard and refrained from comment. "Do you want me to take the boys out for a while to keep them from finding out about the call?" she asked instead.

"No. I'll take them to Dairy Queen. You have to stay and talk to Rafe. You have to tell him he's got to work with Tracey, not against her. You have to tell him not to go to court. You're the only one he'll listen to, Holly. You convinced him to let Kaylin and me keep our jobs at the mall after the trouble in the river, remember? He was going to make us quit and stay in the house all day and night till school started till you explained how it would be counterproductive."

Holly nodded, remembering that particular talk with Rafe. She had used the word counterproductive, though neither Camryn nor Kaylin had been present during the conversation. But it seemed they'd been privy to it, just like this call between Rafe and Tracey Krider.

Her eyes met Camryn's. "I'm very vigilant," Camryn admitted. "I always know what's going on. I have to."

"I understand," said Holly.

And she did. Until coming to live with Rafe, Camryn and Kaylin had been raised by a woman hiding from their father, a woman who had successfully avoided being found for fourteen years. Maintaining vigilance would be extremely important, and old habits die hard.

"But there is one point I'd like to make and it may offend you, Camryn." Holly held her gaze. "You are viewing this as Tracey fighting for her boys against Rafe. A mother and her two children versus a powerful Paradise male. Does anything about this scenario strike you as somewhat familiar?"

"Wow, that's a really shrink-ish observation!" Rather than being offended, Camryn looked delighted. "Except it isn't exactly true, Holly. I'd never want Tracey to keep the boys away from Rafe. Even if they go back to live with her after she dumps the creep, I think Rafe should see a lot of Tony and Trent. Always. He's the closest thing they've ever had for a dad and they need him."

"Do you ever wish that your mother would've let you know your father?" Holly asked curiously. She braced herself for a zealous harangue condemning the late Ben Paradise.

"Sometimes," Camryn replied matter-of-factly. "But Mom got kind of nuts any time his name was mentioned so Kaylin and I never talked about him. I looked at all Rafe's pictures of our dad when I first came here. There were pictures of him with me and Kaylin when we were just babies. He seemed like an okay guy, I guess."

"You've never admitted that to Rafe or Flint or Eva," Holly observed.

"Flint and Eva practically foam at the mouth whenever Kaylin and me trash Ben Paradise. It's fun to watch." Camryn grinned. "Hey, don't pretend you wouldn't do the same if you could, Holly. You don't like the Evil Twin and Evita, either."

"That's not exactly true," Holly argued weakly. "I don't want to make that judgment because I don't know them very well."

"Well, they judged you—and they don't like you!" Camryn exclaimed jovially. "Eva is afraid of you. She whines to Rafe about what will happen if she's assigned to one of your patients during her psychiatry rotation. She's sure you'll make her life a living hell because she thinks you're crazy. A true follow-the-comet nutcase.''

"But why?" Holly was perplexed—and a bit insulted.

"'Cause you're friends with Kaylin and me. You'd have to be crazy to like us, right? Flint is sure you're a militant radical feminist who's taking sides with me and Kaylin 'cause you plan to help us get control of the shares in Paradise Outdoors that our father left us.''

"Have you considered a career with the CIA?" Holly asked mildly. "You do have a way of ferreting out information.''

She was dismayed. Flint and Eva had seemed aloof and stand-offish the few times she'd seen them this past month, but she hadn't taken it personally. Though they had avoided talking to her and directed furtive glances her way, she'd thought them shy and perhaps a bit socially inept. Now it seemed that their withdrawal was actually resentment. Her expression must have reflected her thoughts because Camryn gave her arm an encouraging pat.

"Don't feel bad about those two geeks. They hate all the really cool people. Could I use your car to take the kids out, Holly? If we leave now, you can talk to Rafe when he hangs up.'' Camryn grimaced. "He'll be in a terrible mood and if he tells the boys about Tracey's call while he's mad, it'll come out all wrong. They shouldn't be around till he cools off. You need time to work your shrink magic and calm him down.''

Holly considered it. The girl had made some valid points. "If I let you have the car, you have to promise that you won't do anything foolish, Camryn. That you'll take the boys straight to the Dairy Queen and not go anywhere near the river or—''

Camryn sighed. "I am so over being lectured about that stupid river.''

"How many times do I have to say it?" Rafe's voice rose loud enough for them to hear all the way downstairs. He sounded angry and impatient and frustrated. All the makings for a terrible mood.

"I think you should take the kids out for ice cream right now, Camryn," Holly said decisively. "My door is unlocked and you know where the car keys are. Take a ten dollar bill from my wallet, too. It's upstairs in—''

"I know where it is," Camryn assured her.

Rafe's young wards spent a lot of time at her place and after listening to Camryn's various reports, Holly guessed the inquisitive teen knew where everything she owned was kept. A somewhat daunting thought.

The four kids left moments later, the boys blissfully unaware that Rafe was arguing with their mother about them. Holly walked tentatively up the stairs. She reached his bedroom and was about to knock on the closed door when Rafe opened it. She noticed the receiver was back in its cradle on the nightstand beside the bed. The acrimonious phone call was over.

A smile swept across Rafe's face at the sight of her, his eyes brightening, his expression abruptly transformed from angry to happy. Holly's spirits soared. Rafe usually acknowledged her presence with a nod or a quirk of his lips or an arched brow or two. But right now he was grinning broadly, openly glad to see her.

For one heart-stopping moment, Holly thought he was going to open his arms to her. She knew she would've walked right into them.

But he stood still, his arms at his sides. "I thought you were going to spend the evening making potato salad for the Steens' barbecue. Need to borrow an ingredient or two?"

"No." Holly knew what she was about to say would wipe that wonderful smile from his face. She was loathe to do it but she had to, of course. Rafe was bound to notice that the kids weren't around and Tracey's phone call had to be dealt with.

She looked away from him, focusing on the colorful dream catcher hanging above his bed. She'd been with him and the kids the day he'd purchased five of them at the museum gift shop featuring Native American arts and crafts. Legend had it that the Oneida Indians created the dream catcher, a woven ornament made of beads and a feather which resembled a spider web with a hole in the center. It was to be hung above one's bed to filter dreams. Good dreams passed through to the sleeper while bad ones were trapped there to perish in the light of dawn.

Rafe had given one to Holly and each of the kids, and Tony had insisted that Rafe buy one for himself.

"You need to get your bad dreams catched, too, Rafe," the little boy had said earnestly. Humoring him, Rafe bought another and hung it above his bed.

Holly thought of her own dream catcher above her bed, and then about the erotic dreams she'd been having since moving next door to Rafe Paradise. A flush stained her cheeks. Her dream catcher might be a filter but it was definitely not a censor!

Rafe's dark eyes narrowed as he studied Holly's face. "Is something the matter, Holly?"

"Camryn asked to borrow my car to take the boys out for ice cream," she began.

Rafe gave a bark of laughter. "She must be suffering a creative block, her tales are usually more original than that." He took a step closer. "Was she all sound and fury when you said no? Poor Holly." He touched her cheek. "I'm sorry if she hurt your feelings."

Holly took a deep breath. Though he touched her often, light casual touches with no sexual connotation or follow-up, her responses were always strongly sensual and made her long for more. Thankfully, she'd been able to keep that a secret from him.

Now her body tightened as tiny darts of pleasure skimmed through her. Holly concentrated on keeping her breathing regular. "Rafe, I thought maybe—"

"You're not going to suggest that Camryn be allowed to use your car tonight?" Rafe interrupted incredulously.

"Well, I—"

"You know she's restricted to the house unless she's scheduled to work at the mall, Holly." His face hardened. "She and Kaylin are grounded socially until school starts. We agreed it was fair punishment for that river excursion of theirs, remember?"

"Of course I do, but taking the children to the Dairy Queen can hardly be considered a teenage social event."

"Her Dairy Queen story is only a ruse, and a transparent one at that. If you lend her your car she'll head right for that bunch of dimwits and junior criminals she calls friends. Forget it, Holly."

"Rafe, Camryn was worried the boys would hear you arguing with their mother over the phone," Holly said bluntly. "I agreed that she should take them out for a while and give you time to calm down.''

"I am calm!" he roared.

He pushed past her. The silence in the usually noisy duplex was suddenly deafening. Rafe charged down the stairs, Holly not far behind him.

"Where are the kids?" he demanded.

"They left a few minutes ago to get ice cream.'' She wished she'd gone with them. Despite Camryn's faith in her abilities, she possessed no magic for simple resolutions to complex problems.

Dispirited, Holly headed for the front door.

"To get ice cream? You can't actually believe that!'' Rafe, halfway down the hall, suddenly turned around and advanced on her. "Those girls are like prisoners breaking out of jail! Who knows where they'll end up? The possibilities are endless. Camryn might decide it's a perfect night to go over the falls on a surfboard! Damn it, Holly, you've been manipulated by that scheming, little...''

Rafe stopped just as Holly opened the door. "How did she know I was talking to Tracey?" The question finally occurred to him. "I answered the phone and took the call in my room with the door closed.''

"There is little, if nothing, that goes on around here that Camryn doesn't know about," Holly said wryly. "Rafe, her instincts were good on this. She promised to—''

"To what? After spying on me, she promised to be *good* so you handed over your car keys!'' The momentary truce was over, and Rafe was madder than ever. His hands closed over her shoulders. "I'm not buying that, Holly. I'm not stupid, you know.''

She tried to hang on to her patience. Odd that she had a well-spring of endurance for a patient's outburst, but Rafe's angry eruption fueled one of her own.

"What are you having difficulty believing, Rafe?'' she growled through her teeth. "That Camryn is concerned about the boys? That I've been hoodwinked into handing over my car keys?''

"I want to know, exactly what is your agenda, Holly?'' His fingers tightened on her. "I demand to know now.''

Holly sucked in her cheeks. The question would've puzzled her if she hadn't just learned from Camryn that the Evil Twin and Evita were trying to convince their brother that she was a crazed villainess plotting against the beleaguered clan.

Was Rafe beginning to accept his siblings' paranoia as the truth? *Exactly what is your agenda?* His accusation rang in her ears. She imagined a Paradise cabal discussing her, dissecting her, completely misinterpreting her every word and action.

"My agenda?" Holly's temper blazed to flash point. "Okay, I guess it's time I came clean. Being a radical militant feminist, I plan to liberate Camryn and Kaylin from your male oppression. And there's a bonus in it, too, namely, gaining control of the shares in Paradise Outdoors that your father left them. What a good time we'll have wreaking havoc on the company! I can't wait."

She shook off his hands and stormed across the driveway to her half of the duplex, pausing to shout over her shoulder, "Oh, and in my spare time, I intend to ruin Eva's medical career just for the fun of it. That's because I'm crazy and I get a kick out of screwing up people's lives. That is the sole reason why I went into psychiatry, to mess with people's heads. In fact, that's why I befriended you—to make you as crazy as I am!"

She was mad and she was hurt. Holly raced inside, slamming the door firmly behind her. The hell with Rafe Paradise! The hell with them all! She stomped into the kitchen, turned on the faucet full blast, and thrust the blood-tinged potatoes under the gushing water.

They cleaned up nicely, and she began to chop some more. Of course she didn't mean to consign any of the kids to hell, Holly amended her curse. Just Rafe, and his paranoiac brother and sister who thought she was conspiring with two teenagers against them.

Holly seethed. And *she* was supposed to be the crazy one?

Eight

For a full ten minutes Rafe leaned against the doorjamb in the kitchen, watching her whack potatoes and celery into pieces. Was she pretending to be the chief executioner manning a guillotine? It didn't take a whole lot of imagination to guess whose head she had on the block.

Holly didn't know he was here. She hadn't noticed that her front door wasn't set to automatically lock upon closing, and he'd sneaked in moments after she entered, expecting a confrontation with her. Anticipating one.

Instead he found her in the kitchen standing at the sink, totally unaware of his presence. Rafe decided to wait, to plan his next move. She had caught him off guard earlier. Now it was his turn to do the same to her.

Except as he stood there, trying to nurture his righteous wrath, he kept getting distracted. His eyes became riveted to the nape of her neck as she bent her head slightly while she worked. It looked so vulnerable, so slender and ivory soft. He wanted to touch her there, with his fingers, with his lips.

Stifling a groan, Rafe dragged his gaze away. He tried to focus on the clock on the wall, but less than seven seconds later he was staring at Holly's legs, from her slender ankles to the well-shaped curve of her derriere.

She was wearing a denim outfit that looked like shorts and a shirt except it was all one piece with buttons up the front. There were precisely eight metal buttons. He knew because he'd spent a good deal of time today imagining himself unfastening each one. Exposing her to him.

The memory of the one time he had seen her almost naked had been tantalizing him for the past month. In his mind's eye, he easily conjured up a picture of her breasts round and firm in his hands, the narrow hollow of her waist and the smooth creamy skin of her belly. He visualized her sitting astride him wearing those little white panties...

Holly sliced a potato in half with a particularly vicious chop. Rafe started, abruptly jolted out of his fantasy. His movement, though slight, was enough to alert Holly that she was not alone.

She whirled around, gasping at the sight of him. "What are you doing here?"

Rafe shrugged. "The door wasn't locked. I took that as an invitation to come inside."

"Well, you shouldn't have."

"I'm not welcome?"

"No! Get out. Please," she added stiffly, mocking herself even as she said it. *A lady must always be polite to a gentleman.* Some of her early training ran deep.

"Not a chance." Rafe stalled for time. Now what? He should've been working on a plan instead of standing here ravishing her with his eyes.

Heat surged through his body. He was ready, able and eager to ravish her with much more than a gaze. Though he was winging it, there was one thing he was absolutely sure of: he was not going to leave.

An idea struck. "I want to know how you learned vital confidential information about my family."

"Haven't you figured it out yet?" Holly gave a sarcastic laugh. "Okay, I'll tell you. I bugged your house. I know everything that's said and done over there, you're being monitored day and night. I keep my surveillance equipment stashed in the attic and I intend to sell the information to the highest bidder.''

Rafe arched his brows. ''The girl—uh, woman—must be truly ticked off.''

''I'm also crazy. Let's not forget that.''

A smile teased the corners of his mouth. ''Would you consider putting down the knife, Holly?''

She realized she'd been waving it during her angry spiel. ''If that's supposed to be funny—''

''Well, yeah, it was. Unless you actually intend to stab me with it.''

''I'm busy,'' Holly said coldly, turning back to the sink. ''Go away and leave me alone.''

''What if I did, Holly?'' Rafe crossed the kitchen, stopping when he was directly behind her. ''Wouldn't you hate it if I left you alone?''

His voice was low and husky, a seductive growl against Holly's ear. Her fingers tightened around the knife. ''No. It's what I want,'' she insisted.

He was standing so close that his body brushed hers. His palms glided over her upper arms, then lowered to her waist. He locked his wrists around her, laying his hands against her stomach.

''What about what I want?'' Rafe rested his chin on the top of her head.

Holly fought the urge to close her eyes and relax against him. It would be so easy...too easy. The warmth of his body caressed her, permeated her whole being. Her senses were filled with him. She could hear his heart beating in his chest, she could smell the familiar enticing scent of his aftershave.

''You're not mad anymore.'' The realization dawned. She lay the knife aside and turned off the water.

Rafe shook his head, his lips brushing her hair. ''I can't remember why I was mad in the first place.''

''I can.'' She went rigid again. ''You think I have an *agenda* and am plotting to—''

''That's Flint's theory, not mine.'' Rafe tightened his arms around her, splaying his fingers over her belly. He began a slow massage. ''Paradise Outdoors is his whole life, his baby, so to speak. Sometimes he gets a little carried away in regards to it, just like an overprotective parent.''

''It was *you* who asked me what my agenda was tonight, not Flint,'' she reminded him. She struggled a little, but he didn't let her go.

''I wanted a fight. I knew you'd give me one. Does that make any sense?''

Holly stood still, her brow narrowing thoughtfully. ''Actually, it does, taken in context. You'd just ended an upsetting phone call. I heard you yelling at poor Tracey.''

''You don't even know her and you refer to her as 'poor Tracey.' Well, it's true. She is a born victim, so passive and indecisive that she frustrates the hell out of me.''

''Tracey doesn't yell back?'' surmised Holly.

''No, she doesn't. If I get mad at her—and she gives me plenty of cause—Tracey dissolves in a flood of tears. I end up feeling overbearing and cruel.''

''So there you were, seething, and then I showed up.''

''And wow, do you yell back! That's a compliment,'' he added.

Holly took that to mean that he wasn't threatened by a woman who could hold her own with him. It pleased her.

While they talked he continued to lightly caress her, his fingertips stretching and reaching. Holly felt the effects everywhere. She quivered as sparks of sensual fire shot through her, igniting a ferocious need. As if some invisible switch had been flipped, her anger was abruptly transformed into passion.

Now, a wholly different kind of tension vibrated between them. The full force of his arousal throbbed against her, and Holly felt a heady sense of feminine power. It was intoxicating to inspire such unabashed masculine need in Rafe, especially after a lifetime of being Good Buddy Holly, one of the guys, to every man she knew.

''Flint is not going to be happy when he hears that Camryn knows our father left her and Kaylin those shares in the company.'' Rafe's fingers toyed suggestively with the metal buttons on her suit. ''How long has she known?''

''She didn't say,'' Holly murmured.

Her eyelids fluttered shut and she leaned into him with a soft, shuddering sigh. It was hard to concentrate on either Tracey Krider or Paradise Outdoors when Rafe's lips were nibbling along the curve of her neck.

"Knowing Camryn, she found out early on," Rafe said dryly, "especially if she sensed there was something she wasn't supposed to know."

"That sounds right," Holly agreed.

Unable to remain passive for another moment, she turned slowly in his arms, keeping close and brushing against him, her every move a subtle, sexy caress.

She tilted her head and gazed achingly at the sensual curve of his mouth. Her nipples, taut and tingling, grazed the muscular wall of his chest. A liquid heaviness pulsed deep in her abdomen, between her legs...

"Rafe, I don't have an agenda." She couldn't let him go on believing that she was calculating and deceitful.

"I know. But I do, Holly." He lowered his head, touching his lips to hers.

He kissed her gently at first until she moaned and opened her mouth under his. Their tongues touched and teased as the kiss deepened. One kiss blended into another, each becoming longer and more urgent.

Finally, Rafe lifted his lips, pulling back slightly to gaze down at her. Her mouth was moist and softly swollen, her eyes glazed and slumberous. Bedroom eyes, he thought, and stared into them.

"I want you, Holly. I want to make love to you. I've been waiting for the right time, and that is now. We've spent every day together for nearly a whole month and we've certainly seen each other under less than ideal circumstances. You can't say we don't know each other well enough."

Holly twined her arms around his neck, her fingers combing through his sleek dark hair. "No, I guess we can't say that."

Her legs felt weak, and she clung to him for support. Standing required too much energy; she wanted to give in to the delicious lethargy seeping through her and lie down.

"Let me have you, Holly," he rasped, slipping his thigh between hers. She drew a sharp breath as he cupped her intimately. "Right now. No more waiting."

She groaned into his mouth and reached for him, tracing the shape of him with her hand. His body was hard and taut with tension, his skin flushed with desire. Holly acknowledged her excitement and fascination, but she gave up her self-control to love.

"Yes, Rafe, I want you so much."

She was in love with him, she admitted to herself. She trusted him, she respected and admired him. She felt as if she'd spent her entire life waiting for him yet paradoxically, it was as if they had known each other forever. He was truly Mr. Right, and they were together at last. Holly blinked back a surge of emotional tears.

Rafe picked her up and held her high against his chest. He headed out of the kitchen and up the stairs with her in his arms.

"I've never been carried before," Holly murmured, slightly dazed. "It's very romantic. Not to mention slightly unnerving."

"Mmm, not to mention that." Rafe's grin was wickedly bold, his dark eyes glittered with sexual intent.

Holly pressed her face into him. The cotton of his well-worn Minnesota Twins T-shirt was soft against her cheek. He carried her into her bedroom and lay her down on the queen-size bed.

The dream catcher he'd bought her hung over it, swaying and stirring in the light breeze generated from the ceiling fan. Rafe glanced at it. "No bad dreams, I hope?"

Holly dimpled. "It depends on how you interpret the word 'bad.' Because lately I've had some dreams that would make you blush."

Rafe grinned wolfishly. "Not me, baby." He stood beside it and stripped off his T-shirt and jeans while she watched raptly. "I have a confession to make, Holly. When I saw you standing at my bedroom door tonight, the last thing I wanted to do was fight with you. I wanted to do this."

"Me, too," she admitted, breathless, remembering how much she'd wanted to be in his arms.

"No more unresolved sexual issues?" he asked, stepping out of his boxer briefs.

Holly stared at his powerful nude body. "No," she whispered. "They're resolved, Rafe."

It was true. Far from intimidating her, his masculine strength and size thrilled and aroused her. She wanted to make love with the man she loved. Holly was filled with an ardent urgency. She had been waiting a long, long time for this. For him.

Rafe came down to lay beside her. "I need you so badly, Holly."

He unbuttoned the eight metal buttons, bringing his earlier fantasy to life.

Holly assisted him, pulling off the outfit to kneel before him in her navy blue bra and panties. Rafe eyed her avidly, his control beginning to slip.

"I've been waiting for this moment since that first night at the Great Plains Motel, Holly." He reached up to unclip the front fastener of her bra and carefully removed it. Her breasts swung soft and free.

"I didn't want to stop that night but I was too nervous," Holly confessed. "You can't imagine how many times I've relived that night, Rafe."

"With a different outcome?" She nodded her head. "So have I, honey. I've spent the last month torturing myself night after night imagining a *very* different outcome," he added drolly.

"But stopping was the right thing to do, wasn't it, Rafe? You agreed that we were moving too fast and even though—"

"Holly, do you remember when I said you have a tendency to overthink things?" He pulled her down on top of him. "Well, you're doing it again." His hands roved over the length of her smooth, bare back. "I'm going to kiss you to shut you up."

"I think that would probably be a good idea."

His mouth closed fiercely over hers in a possessive kiss that went on and on, a primal oral mating. They were both breathless and panting for air when he finally, reluctantly, lifted his lips from hers.

Rafe held her face in his hands and stared into her soft brown eyes. "I'll make it good for you, Holly, I promise."

"I know." She gazed at him earnestly, needing to be honest. Her lack of experience plagued her. Her long hiatus from sex made her feel very much like an overaged virgin. Rafe had admitted fantasizing about her. What if she didn't live up to expectations? The thought of disappointing him was unbearable.

"I—I really want to make it good for you, Rafe." Holly gulped. "But if I—"

"Relax. You aren't going to be graded on your performance." Rafe smiled. "After all this time, just being inside you is going to be good for me."

Trust Rafe to put things in perspective, Holly mused gratefully. His warm reassurance melted her flare of anxiety.

"So I don't have to do *anything?*" Her eyes held a teasing gleam. "Should I just lie still and mentally list the pros and cons of various serotonin re-uptake inhibitors while you—"

"Oh, you're definitely going to be an active player, sweetie." He laughed softly.

He slipped his hand between her thighs to rub the damp silk of her panties, then removed the lacy scrap to caress her intimately. His touch was electric, and Holly shuddered as intense, exciting sensations bombarded her, clouding her mind, narrowing her consciousness. There was only Rafe, and the rapture induced by his caressing fingers.

She couldn't think, she could only feel as her hips began to move in slow, erotic rhythm. A low moan escaped from her throat, then another. She clutched at him, gasping his name, her movements frantic and eager. The thrill of his touch within her sent shock waves of pleasure crashing through her.

"Let it happen, Holly." His mouth was wet and hot against her neck. "You're so close."

He laved her nipple, then suckled it, and she felt the carnal effects deep within her womb. It was incredible, like nothing she had ever experienced or even dared to imagine. Holly whimpered softly. She felt as if she were enveloped in a white-hot swirling mist of feeling, needing, wanting....

"I'll take care of you, baby." Rafe's voice penetrated the thick, sensual fog. "Just let go."

Control slipped away completely and she suddenly shattered, coming hard against his hand. She tumbled into dark, blissful oblivion and lay quietly in the glowing warmth, floating mindlessly for what seemed to be a long, long time.

Finally her eyes drifted open. Rafe was holding her, watching her, his gaze intent. He smiled at her and she blushed.

"I—I don't know what to say, Rafe," she said huskily.

"You could say that you weren't lying there mentally listing the pros and cons of sero-whatever-they-are," he suggested.

"Rafe, you can believe me when I tell you that I couldn't have named a single serotonin re-uptake inhibitor if my life depended on it."

They both laughed.

"You're beautiful, Holly," he said warmly.

"So are you." She cupped his sex, entranced by the soft weight, then ran her fingers along the smooth, virile length of him. "I didn't wait for you," she murmured.

Their eyes met.

"I didn't want you to." He dipped his head and kissed her. "We're not on any kind of formal timetable here, Holly. And we're not keeping score. Okay?"

She nodded tremulously. "Okay."

Feeling bold, Holly leaned up to reach into the drawer of the octagonal nightstand adjacent to the bed. She pulled out a foil packet. "Remember this? You gave it to me that night at the motel. For safekeeping, you said."

"For keeping safe." He took the small square foil. "Are the other ones in that drawer, too?"

Holly nodded, watching as he sheathed himself.

"Good." His dark eyes blazed. "We'll be using them."

He settled between her legs and rose above her, big and strong and powerful. Slowly, carefully, he entered her. Stretched and filled her. Holly lifted her hands to hold him more firmly against her, then arched her hips to take him deeper.

Never had she been so aware of his strength, so overwhelmed by it. Wildly and deeply aroused by it. She concentrated on the feel of him inside her. Thick and hard and tight.

"A perfect fit," Rafe growled.

"I was thinking exactly the same thing." Her hands tightened around him possessively.

"Of course you were, sweetheart. Great minds and all that..."

Pure unadulterated happiness flooded her. Their bodies were joined. He was a part of her and belonged to her in a way no other man ever had or would. "I love you, Rafe."

The words slipped out but she didn't regret them. It felt good telling him even if he didn't say it back. She wanted him to know.

He began to move within her, his strokes long and slow and deep. The sensations enthralled her. Holly held on tight as the erotic rhythm grew faster and gathered intensity. He thrust harder and she matched his movements in counterpoint as an exquisite tension began to shimmer and build within her.

She hadn't expected to find release again but she was swept along in a wild sensual torrent that lifted her higher and higher. When Rafe uttered a low guttural cry and buried himself in her again and again, her body spasmed in ecstasy along with his.

Finally, he collapsed against her, pressing gentle kisses to her cheek, to her throat and shoulder. Tenderly, she smoothed her hands over the damp skin of his back. They lay together in the sweet languid aftermath. Neither felt the need to talk. Words seemed unnecessary, almost an intrusion.

Holly couldn't remember ever feeling so very close, so utterly attuned to anyone. In contrast to what she shared with Rafe, her relationship with Devlin Brennan seemed so very incomplete. Amazing that for years she had deluded herself about being in love with Dev. Though she'd really had no basis for comparison, Holly reminded herself. Until Rafe, she had never been in love before.

The sudden shrill ring of the telephone seemed to come from some other dimension, jarring them both out of their languorous dreamworld.

Rafe resented it greatly. "Don't answer it, Holly. You're not on call this weekend."

"What if it's Camryn?"

"Let your answering machine pick up. If it's Camryn or a genuine emergency, then get on the line."

Holly nodded her compliance. After six rings, the answering machine on the bedside table clicked on.

"Hi, Holly. Collin here," said a deep male voice. "Just checking in. I'd ask you to call me back but I know you won't, so I'll call later. 'Bye."

Holding him in her arms, Holly felt the tension sweep Rafe's body. She tightened her arms protectively. "That was Collin Widmark."

Rafe wondered if the whites of his eyes had turned a bright color of green because the wave of jealousy crashing over him was so strong that tangible evidence of his condition seemed entirely likely.

Collin Widmark. "Dr. Widmark's kid," he said through his teeth.

"Kid?" Holly echoed, smiling. "I think he's around your age, Rafe. Maybe even a little older."

"Does he call you often?" Rafe was unable to lie still. He thrashed around, snatching the pillows and propping them against the headboard of the bed, then sat up with them at his back. "That call doesn't seem like the first one from him." He'd noticed that the *eligible bachelor son of Holly's boss* hadn't bothered to add his surname. The weasel.

"It's not. Collin Widmark is living, breathing proof that in some instances *The Rules* really work."

"And that would mean?" Rafe demanded tightly.

"That being elusive spurs certain guys into being persistent." Holly scooted up and cuddled close to him, draping one arm across his stomach. He remained stiff and unresponsive.

She was undeterred, stringing a trail of little kisses along his collarbone, from his shoulder to his neck. His skin tasted salty. Indescribably delicious. The old advertising jingle played through her mind and she smiled softly. It was apt.

"You're saying that jerk is pursuing you?"

"I think it must have a lot to do with ego. Collin Widmark is very spoiled from all the attention he's received from women, and he can't believe that one would have no interest in going out with him. Which I don't," Holly added pointedly.

"So the spoiled smarmy jackal can't take no for an answer?"

"Collin thinks I'm playing hard to get—he actually told me that—so he keeps calling. Not that he's stalking me or anything like that," she hastened to add, prompted by Rafe's thunderous expression.

His arms finally came around to encircle her. "You've never mentioned him before."

"What's to say?" Holly grinned up at him. "Are you jealous? I think I'm flattered."

"Damn it, Holly, this isn't funny. I don't want some toad calling you."

She gave a yelp of laughter. "I bet that's the first time anybody has ever referred to Collin Widmark as a toad! I know he sees himself as a handsome prince."

"But you don't." Rafe felt himself relax a little. Holly's lighthearted responses were reassuring, although the urge to pummel Collin Widmark for daring to call her was still rather appealing.

Holly gave him an affectionate squeeze. "I certainly don't."

"The guy drives a fire-engine-red Porsche, Holly," Rafe admitted reluctantly. Toad or jackal or a beastly combination, young Widmark did have great taste in cars.

Her smile widened. "That's nice for him, but do you really think I care what kind of a car a man drives, Rafe?"

"Well, no," he conceded. After all, she'd just gone to bed with a man who drove four kids around in a Jeep Grand Cherokee and had chosen not to answer the call of the Porsche owner.

Still, Rafe vividly remembered that day when Holly had announced she intended to have a full social life here in Sioux Falls. He had decided then and there to sabotage her plans and he had. Quite successfully, too. He and the kids had ensnared her in the tangle of their lives, monopolizing her, leaving her no time for anybody else but them. When she wasn't seeing patients, she was with her next-door neighbors.

Occasionally, Rafe pondered the strange turn fate had taken. The kids' presence in his life had worked against him with other women who viewed them as interferences or complications they would rather not take on. But Holly's professional interest in working with youngsters had given him an inside track with her personally.

The kids genuinely liked Holly; they trusted and accepted her. Rafe had taken full advantage, encouraging them to involve her in their lives. Which they had. Camryn and Kaylin borrowed her car to get to and from their jobs at the mall. If the girls were watching something on TV at a time the boys wanted to watch something else, one group or the other headed to Holly's to commandeer her television set.

Spending so much time together had naturally led to sharing responsibilities. Rafe consulted her for her opinions and advice. The ever-conscientious Holly took her role in the kids' lives seriously. She'd volunteered to stay with them during the two overnight business trips Rafe took this past month, she was around to supervise whenever he had evening meetings with clients.

Life was far more peaceful since she'd entered their lives. His young half sisters couldn't get into as much trouble with two adults in charge working together as a team. Rafe never hesitated to point that out to Holly.

He felt no guilt in using the kids to bind her closely to him. He'd intended to have her from that first frustrating night at the Great Plains Motel, and if she needed time, he was willing to give it to her. What he wasn't willing to do was to compete with the bachelors of Sioux Falls for her attention. Jokers like Collin Widmark could not be allowed near her.

"When did Widmark start calling you?" Rafe asked, once again scowling at the unmitigated gall of the other man. Holly was his!

"You're as tenacious as my mom on certain subjects," sighed Holly, lying against him, her head resting on his shoulder. She idly traced his flat male nipple with her finger. "Collin came to the Widmark office suite on one of my first days there and started calling soon after. I always told him no, Rafe. I was never once tempted to say yes. Now, is the inquisition over?"

"Definitely. Who wants to waste time talking about an insufferable pinhead like Widmark?"

Holly managed to keep a straight face. "My thoughts exactly."

He lowered his head to kiss her. She responded warmly, but when he would have deepened the kiss in arousing passion, she turned her head slightly, brushing her lips against his cheek.

"Rafe, about Tracey..."

"I don't want to talk about her, either." Rafe tried to capture her mouth.

"It's important, Rafe."

"Honey, I'm not going to fight with you."

"Good, because I don't want to fight." She dodged his seeking mouth once again. "Does Tracey want to break up with her child-hating boyfriend?"

Rafe sat up straight, his dark eyes turning cold. "So she says. Tonight, anyway. Who knows what she'll feel like doing tomorrow? Her timing for this fairy tale about all of them living together and being a family again couldn't be worse, coming right before school starts. She hasn't seen the kids since the Fourth of July, and now this."

"But is it a fairy tale?" Holly shifted to face him. "If Tracey wants her children—"

"Does she want them enough to end things with the boyfriend? I doubt it. She told me she was *thinking* about kicking him out, she hasn't done it yet."

"Maybe she needs an incentive to do it. Getting her children back would—"

"What Tracey needs isn't the issue here. When she signed over guardianship of the boys to me I made it clear that the kids' lives weren't going to be continually disrupted by shipping them from place to place on a whim. A friend of mine who specializes in custody cases drew up the guardianship agreement. It'll hold up in court."

"Not that Tracey could afford a court fight with you."

"Don't try and make Tracey the sympathetic underdog here, Holly. She has terrible judgment and even less common sense. She gave up her kids for a bum she'd known less than a couple months."

"When the boys came here, was it the first time they weren't with their mother or were they regularly sent to live with other people?" asked Holly.

Rafe leaned heavily against the headboard. "This was the first time."

"And before that, during the years you acted as Trent's Big Brother, did you notice any signs of abuse or neglect?"

"Of course not!" Rafe was indignant. "I would've taken action if I had!"

"Of course you would have," Holly agreed. "I'm just trying to point out that Trent and Tony are loving, adaptable little boys and they wouldn't be if they'd been abused and neglected by their mother all those years before moving in with you."

Rafe folded his arms and glared at her. "You sound like a damn shrink, Holly."

"Thanks," she replied sweetly. "Let me return the compliment. You sound like a damn lawyer, Rafe."

He tried hard to stoke his righteous anger. "Tracey's children are in danger from her boyfriend who has an explosive temper and does not like kids. Hell, she admits that herself. That's why she sent the boys away."

"But if she's willing to break up with the boyfriend, shouldn't she be encouraged to do it? Threatening to take her to court in a custody fight only encourages her to stay in a destructive abusive relationship with the man."

"Holly—"

"The bond between a mother and child is one of the deepest and strongest there is, Rafe. If Tony and Trent want to be with their mother, and she wants them to—"

"Holly, this is not a psychological case study," Rafe huffed impatiently. "And Tracey Krider is not one of your patients."

"She could be." Holly's brown eyes glowed. "Our goals in therapy would be to bolster her resolve to break up with the boyfriend and to reunite her family. We'd work on making her a strong, independent woman instead of a passive victim."

"She couldn't afford your rates, Doc."

"She could if I donated my time. I'd be working—what do lawyers call it, pro bono?"

Rafe stared at her. "You'd do that, wouldn't you?"

"I want to help Trent and Tony and that means helping their mother. You feel the same way, Rafe."

"You're giving me way too much credit, Holly," he mumbled. "Tracey drives me crazy."

"But you're committed to helping her, anyway. You don't turn your back on people, you don't quit to take the easy way out. That's why you're such a good man, Rafe. The best man I know."

She felt as if her heart would burst with love for him. And that love was a many-faceted one, combining friendship, admiration, common goals. And passion, a burning, hungry passion.

Desire and need flooded her. She didn't think it was possible to want him again so soon after being thoroughly sated by their lovemaking, yet she did. She wanted him even more because now she knew exactly what she'd been missing. The closeness, both physical and emotional, the pleasure, the satisfaction.

She needed it. She needed him.

Holly climbed onto his lap and their mouths fused in a long, hot kiss. She clung to him, moaning softly as she sank her nails into the hard muscles of his shoulders. She could feel Rafe surging against her, and his urgency fueled her own.

"Rafe, please," she cried. The feel of his hands all over her body was driving her out of her mind. "I want you inside me. I don't want to wait another minute."

Her words went to his head like a shot of hundred-proof whiskey. "No waiting," he promised. But he cared too much not to take the time to protect her, so he reached into the drawer, holding her astride him with his other arm.

His fingers closed around a foil packet at the moment that the sound of car doors slamming outside broke the late summer stillness. The voices of Camryn, Kaylin, Trent and Tony grew louder as they emerged from Holly's car.

Holly and Rafe looked at each other and groaned.

"Camryn said she'd take the kids straight to the Dairy Queen and then come back." Holly reluctantly slid off Rafe's lap. "Seems like that's exactly what she did."

"I can't believe it." Rafe's whole body was throbbing with unslaked need. "The one time she doesn't stay out until all hours is the one time I wouldn't have minded if she did. My little sister has a real talent for being inconsistently inconsistent."

Holly wondered if Rafe noticed that he'd omitted the definitive "half" in referring to Camryn. She gazed lovingly at him as she quickly pulled on her clothes. "I'll go check on the kids. You don't have to hurry. Take your time."

"What I'll take is a cold shower." Rafe swung his legs over the side of the bed. "One is definitely required. And, Holly..."

His voice stopped her on her way out of the bedroom. The way he was looking at her made her ache with yearning.

"I'll be back later tonight," he said, his soft, sexy voice warm with promise. He reached up to give the dream catcher a swat. "To act out some of those bad girl dreams of yours."

The thumping on the downstairs wall began—the boys with a ball? Camryn with the bat?—and Holly dragged herself out of the bedroom. Rafe went directly into the shower stall and turned on the taps.

Later, he returned to re-create some deliciously bad dreams of his own with her.

Nine

"I'm not sure I heard you correctly, Rafe." Flint Paradise sat behind his desk in his office at the Paradise Outdoors headquarters. Rafe occupied the serviceable wooden chair nearby. "Run it by me again, okay?"

Flint's wasn't the typical spacious corner office of the CEO of a successful company. His office was small-to-the-point-of-cramped and located in the interior of the building. There wasn't a single window to break the monotony of the beige-painted walls and the furnishings were equally dull and Spartan, without even a hint of luxury.

Absently, Rafe studied the posters on the wall, all of them picturing the first-rate hunting, fishing, camping and other outdoor gear sold by Paradise Outdoors. The product posters were the only bit of color to brighten the drabness of the decor. The office mirrored Flint's own single-mindedness. Flint was Paradise Outdoors. His passion and interest in the company was all-consuming.

No wonder his brother was having difficulty fathoming the request that had been made of him, Rafe mused without rancor. He had no doubts that Flint had heard correctly the first time, but it took him a while to process anything unrelated to Paradise Outdoors. Asking his twin had been a long shot, but at Holly's suggestion he'd decided to give it a try.

"Okay, here goes," he said patiently. "I'm going to a wedding—"

"You're going to a family wedding in Michigan with Holly Casale," Flint interjected, repeating what he'd already been told twice. Except he made it sound like Rafe was headed to a cell on death row. "And you want me to stay at your place with those kids while you're gone?" Flint's voice rose on a note of incredulity. His tone clearly implied that being strapped into a malfunctioning electric chair would be preferable.

"It's just for a weekend. We'd leave Friday afternoon and come back Sunday," Rafe attempted to sound reassuring.

"Going to a family wedding with a woman is dangerous, Rafe," warned Flint. "Everybody gets the wrong idea, especially the family and the woman."

"Look, I'm not crazy about the idea myself but I already promised to go. If I don't, Holly will have to endure another of her family's matchmaking efforts. She heard from her cousin, the bride, that the new candidate is a shy forty-seven-year-old chiropractor who still lives with his mother."

"Yeah, but if you go to the wedding her family will think *you're* the new candidate!"

"Holly and I are prepared to ignore that. We both know I'm there to save her from a weekend with the mama's boy."

"Well, I'll be spending the entire weekend right here at Paradise Outdoors," said Flint. "We're installing a new inventory system. It's state-of-the-art, Rafe. Do you want to look over the information packet?"

"No, I'll take your word that it's the best. For Paradise Outdoors, you wouldn't settle for anything less." Rafe heaved a resigned sigh. "I guess it goes without saying that you won't stay with the kids, either?"

"Either? Did you already ask Eva and get turned down?"

"I thought about it but decided not to ask her. She'd just say no."

"True. Although, even if she were to agree it wouldn't be a good idea. Putting Eva, Camryn and Kaylin under one roof for even a couple hours is risky."

"I know." Rafe rubbed his temples with his fingertips. "They'd never last through a sisterly weekend together. Somebody would surely implode. Probably Eva."

"If you're bound and determined to go to this wedding, you could always leave the kids alone," suggested Flint. "You've done it before."

"Not for a while." Not since Holly had moved in next door nearly two months ago, to be precise. "And never for a whole weekend."

"Well, what about the boys' mother? Didn't you say she was visiting more regularly? Why can't she stay with her own kids?"

"Holly is working with Tracey and has set up a visitation schedule with the boys that she is following faithfully. But she still hasn't kicked out her scumbag boyfriend. I can't risk putting Tracey in charge of anyone until she gets him out of her life for good."

"Anyway, Tracey's no match for Camryn and Kaylin." Flint smirked. "It'd be like sending a chicken to watch a pair of wolverines."

"You have a point." Rafe picked up the geopositional satellite locator that lay on the desktop. The device signaled the carrier's geographical position anywhere in the world. It was superior to a compass, one of the new high-tech entries in the Paradise Outdoors inventory.

"Uh, I heard about Camryn's latest stunt at the high school," Flint said casually.

"Would that be the one where she lay down on top of the vice-principal's car parked alongside the building? After she talked some kids in the class into telling the overexcitable school librarian that she'd jumped out the window?"

"That would be it." Flint actually laughed. "I remember that librarian, Miss Hinsley. She was around back in our day. Very tightly wound."

"It's not funny," growled Rafe. "Camryn lay there on top of the car, pretending to be unconscious. Poor Miss Hinsley thought she'd jumped from the third floor and went into hysterics. Camryn didn't move a muscle the whole time. The little wretch didn't give it up till the paramedics arrived. Then she started laughing.''

Rafe winced at the memory of the outraged phone calls generated by his little sister's awful prank. ''Camryn couldn't figure out why everybody got so mad at her, why the police threatened to bring charges against her. She said nobody in this town has a sense of humor.''

''Well, it is kind of humorous that her performance was believable enough to trick the school staff into summoning help. Especially considering that Camryn is notorious there for stirring things up. Not that I approve of what she did,'' Flint added quickly as Rafe's face darkened. ''Er, what did your friend Holly have to say about it?''

''She and Camryn had a confidential talk. They have a lot of them. Holly also talked to the cops, the paramedics, and the principal. No charges were filed, though Camryn has after-school detention for a month. Holly has a very calming way about her. I wouldn't have handled the situation as well.'' A definite understatement there, Rafe acknowledged. Thank God Holly had willingly stepped in and taken over.

''You're getting in awfully deep with that girl, Rafe.'' Flint looked troubled.

''Woman,'' Rafe corrected automatically.

''That woman's spun a web around you that would do a black widow spider proud, Rafe. Eva and I were talking about it just the other day. Holly Casale is in league with those little brats, and they're working together to turn you against us.''

Rafe groaned. ''No more conspiracy theories, please!''

Flint lapsed into silence. Rafe stared at his brother. He regretted the growing distance between the two of them. Between the three of them, because Eva was aloof and irritable with him, as well. Unfortunately, the gulf created by Camryn and Kaylin's arrival last year had been widened by Holly's presence.

Flint and Eva resented the intrusion into their longtime, tightly knit trio and in protest had relegated themselves to outsider status in their brother's life. At least, that was Holly's professional take on the current Paradise dynamics.

Rafe knew his brother and sister were wrong about Holly, though. Far from trying to turn him against them, she was always suggesting that he make friendly overtures to Flint and Eva. Holly wanted everybody to be one big happy family, including Tracey Krider, and though Rafe admired her optimism, he didn't share it.

This meeting with Flint was a case in point.

"I guess it won't be long before you and Holly Casale are making plans for your own wedding," Flint said gloomily.

"That's ridiculous!" Rafe laughed. "We've never discussed marriage. Things are good between us just the way they are. Why would we want to screw it up by getting married?"

"Have you ever asked her that question?" When Rafe shook his head no, Flint smiled cynically. "Maybe you should. Because I think she would have a totally different answer. All women want to get married, Rafe. They're genetically programmed into it."

"That is such a vast overgeneralization! Eva—"

"Right now Eva is concentrating on her career, so she's put those needs on hold. *Temporarily.*" Flint paused for emphasis, then resumed his discourse. "Holly Casale undoubtedly did the same while she was busy getting her M.D. But now she's got it, and those inborn wifely and maternal instincts of hers are kicking in. And there you are, my brother, living right next door to her. You even supply the kids, although she really must be desperate to be willing to take on *those* kids. Still, she probably figures they're a means to the end—getting herself a wedding ring and a baby."

"You're a first-rate businessman, but stay away from the field of behavioral science, Flint," Rafe advised his brother. "Your theories are half baked, at best. Idiotic, at worst."

"You hope." Flint shrugged. "So what are you going to do about the kids while you're at the wedding?"

"Take them along."

"To Michigan? You're kidding!"

"Do I look like I'm kidding, Flint?"

"No, you look mighty grim. But I guess there is an up side to this for you. After Holly's family meet Camryn and Kaylin, chances are good that you'll be disqualified as marriageable material—since they'll be getting a firsthand look at our frightening gene pool and all.''

Flint was laughing as his twin brother left his office. Rafe didn't crack a smile.

When he thought of what lay ahead, he grew grimmer still. He wasn't keen on the idea of attending this family wedding in the first place, given what he'd learned from Holly about her relatives' propensity for matchmaking.

Admittedly, he had suffered a jealous pang or two—or maybe even three—at the thought of someone like Collin Widmark making a play for Holly, but the reclusive chiropractor in Michigan did not strike him as a romantic threat. Though he would miss Holly that weekend, Rafe hadn't even thought of coming along to her cousin's wedding.

But then she had asked him to. While lying in bed after an earth-shattering session of lovemaking. How could he refuse her anything in that blissed-out state of perfect fusion? He had even insisted on paying for the four kids' plane tickets in the likely case that Flint and Eva would refuse to stay with them. It made sense for him to pay, he'd said, because with his successful law practice and lucrative shares in Paradise Outdoors, his income was substantially higher than hers.

But in the light of day, and minus that rapturous afterglow, Rafe began to have second thoughts. His doubts multiplied after his troubling talk with his twin. No one knew better than Holly how disruptive those four kids could be, yet she was willing— even eager—to expose them to her family during the hysteria of a wedding. In an attempt to incorporate *everybody* into one big happy family?

Suddenly nothing was making much sense at all.

Rafe chided himself for letting Flint get into his head. Holly was *not* laying the groundwork to trap him into marriage, he assured himself.

Nevertheless he found himself contemplating the meeting with his brother later that evening when he and Holly were enjoying a kid-free respite in his kitchen. Camryn and Kaylin were in their bedroom, presumably doing homework, the sound of their atrocious music filtering downstairs. Trent and Tony were in bed, having completed their homework with the usual daily assistance from Rafe and Holly.

They had a very workable arrangement: Rafe helped the boys with math, Holly with spelling and social studies. Neither child liked sitting still for long and engaging their interest in schoolwork wasn't easy, though the one-on-one attention worked far better than Rafe's solitary efforts last year.

Holly had also worked out some kind of deal with the girls involving points, homework, and driving her car. Miraculously, it seemed to be working. Even better, he wasn't involved in it so he didn't always have to threaten and nag.

An infinite improvement over last year, which blurred in his memory as a chaotic, unceasing nightmare. Having Holly around had made an enormous difference for all of them, Rafe acknowledged as he watched her sip a glass of iced tea.

She probably figures those kids are a means to the end—getting herself a wedding ring and a baby. Flint's snide allegation suddenly echoed in his head.

"Flint thinks that your family will start planning our wedding, given their obsession with marriage." Rafe stared at her intently. "I assured him that you are as uninterested in getting married as I am."

His words hit Holly with sledgehammer force. *Uninterested in getting married?* Where had he gotten that idea? True, she and Rafe had never discussed marriage—except to joke about her family's attempts to marry her off to all the wrong men—but never had she declared herself uninterested in marriage.

In fact, she thought about it now more than she ever had before because Rafe Paradise was the one man in the world that she wanted to marry.

But he was uninterested in marrying her! Holly took a big gulp of tea. This was the first time she'd heard that, and it was a revelation. So many responses came to mind....

She could say that he'd neglected to mention he was *uninterested in marrying her* when he took her to bed every night. That he hadn't brought up the fact that he was *uninterested in marrying her* when she arranged her afternoon patient schedule to accommodate driving the younger children to their various activities and appointments—thus freeing him from the role of chauffeur—or when she allowed his half sisters to borrow her car.

She might point out that he had not said he was *uninterested in marrying her* when he had turned over the daily chore of providing dinner, either by cooking or ordering take-out, to her. He insisted on paying the food bills, but took no responsibility for providing the meals. She'd freely taken on the task, Holly admitted to herself. She certainly expected no rewards and yet...

She certainly hadn't expected to hear him baldly announce that he was *uninterested in marrying her!*

Holly stared blindly at the striped wallpaper, her mind spinning in confusion. She wasn't doing all those things for him and the children to wring a marriage proposal from Rafe Paradise. Was she? *Or was she?*

"Holly?" His voice filled her head. She turned her head to look at him.

Their eyes met. He was watching her, his expression decidedly grim.

Holly pulled herself together. "I'm sorry, my mind was drifting," she heard herself say.

"In the middle of our conversation?"

He actually looked hurt. Was she supposed to be hanging on his every word? Holly fumed. A mortifying thought struck her. Is that what she usually did? Hang on his every word like a lovestruck fool? Maybe he thought the two of them could have a good laugh over how uninterested he was in marrying her. Some joke. It was on her!

She strove for at least a semblance of pride. "I'm concerned about a patient who is dangerously suicidal." Holly turned professional, an area where she was nobody's fool. "This patient has an abandonment complex and took the news that I would be away for the weekend as a personal rejection. I'm not sure I should leave her to attend Heidi's wedding."

Rafe visibly relaxed, and a cold anger seeped through her. He didn't care that she had made no reply to his antimarriage declaration. He wasn't even going to question her story. He was simply relieved to drop the subject of marriage altogether.

Holly stood up. "On the other hand, I did promise my family

that I would be there and I want to see little Heidi get married, so I suppose I'll end up going.''

"What about your patient with the abandonment complex?''

Like he cared! Holly's smile was very forced. "I'll assure her that I'm not abandoning her and if I feel she is a danger to herself, I'll hospitalize her before I leave." Which is what she would do if said patient actually existed.

Holly glanced at her watch, something of an unnecessary gesture because the wall clock was directly in front of her. "Oh, I forgot. I'm expecting a call from my sister. I'd better get over to my place so I don't miss it.''

Rafe rose to his feet. He didn't want her to go. "You can call her from here.''

"I am willing to bet next month's rent that either Camryn or Kaylin is on the phone.'' Holly kept her smile in place, though she felt as if her face was going to crack from the strain.

Rafe lifted the receiver on the kitchen extension.

"Excuse me, I'm using the phone!'' Camryn's voice, annoyed and impatient, sounded loudly over the line.

"I thought you were doing your homework,'' countered Rafe.

"I am.'' Camryn was peeved. "Over the phone. Now, hang up, Rafe.''

Holly headed out of the kitchen. Rafe followed her. "Call from here, Holly. Camryn is no more doing homework than—''

"I'd rather go home, Rafe.'' Holly was walking so fast she was already at the front door.

He caught her wrist, halting her before she could walk out. "Holly, I don't want you to go.''

He was accustomed to spending the evening with her. They either read or watched TV or talked until the kids were in bed for the night. And then they went over to her place where they could be wonderfully, hungrily, urgently alone...

Holly knew the itinerary he had planned for them by the purposeful expression on his face, by the glint in his eyes. She rebelled. It would be difficult enough to endure watching a rerun of "Seinfeld" with a man who'd announced that he found the idea of marrying her repugnant. Going to bed with him was out of the question.

"Rafe, I need some time alone." She tried to disengage her wrist.

Instead of letting her go, he pulled her closer. "I'll come with you. We don't have to wait until the girls are in bed. I want to be alone with you, too, sweetheart."

Holly marveled at how completely he'd managed to miss the point. Her facade of normalcy, already shaky, collapsed. "I meant, alone, as in by myself, in a solitary state. I haven't spent an evening alone since I set foot in Sioux Falls," she added, astonished by the sudden realization.

It had seemed so natural to be with Rafe and/or the kids that she hadn't been aware of how completely they filled her time. And her life. Holly yanked her arm free. "I'm leaving, Rafe."

"Okay, go home and talk to your sister." Rafe was clearly baffled by her uncharacteristic lack of compliance and amiability. "I'll be over around eleven. Or ten?" He sounded hopeful.

"No. Not anytime tonight."

"But—"

"Rafe, don't be so—so needy!" Holly stormed from the premises while he was still reeling from the charge she'd hurled at him.

Needy? Him? He watched her disappear inside her half of the duplex, heard her front door close. Shock was replaced by humiliation—*him, needy?*—and then displaced by a fierce wave of outrage. *He was not needy!*

Rafe slammed the door hard, then turned to find himself facing Kaylin who stood at the bottom of the staircase.

"Uh-oh, trouble in Paradise?" Kaylin regarded him archly.

"None of your business! I don't want to talk about it."

She shrugged and walked past him toward the kitchen.

Rafe followed. "How much did you hear?" he demanded, contradicting himself.

"Not too much. Just you mercilessly hounding Holly so much that you got on her last nerve and she took off."

"That is not true!"

"Sure it is." Kaylin opened the refrigerator and idly surveyed the contents.

"Did you and Camryn do anything or say anything to upset Holly?"

"It isn't us, Rafe, it's you." Kaylin heaved a knowing sigh. "Men never give women a break, our mom said so. She said they—"

"I don't care to hear what your mother said, Kaylin. And if it has anything to do with men, you'd do well to forget it because Marcine Paradise was hardly an authority on the subject."

"Like you're such an authority on women?" Kaylin was scornful. "Jeez, Rafe, you sure blew it. Since you managed to get Holly, I thought maybe you knew what you were doing but it looks like you're just as dysfunctional as Flint and Eva." She rolled her wide, dark eyes. "*They* couldn't get a date to save their lives."

Rafe pushed the refrigerator door closed, nearly catching Kaylin's head in it.

"Stop wasting time and go back up and finish your homework, Kaylin."

"I'm not saying that me and Camryn aren't dysfunctional, too." Kaylin attempted to be conciliatory. "'Cause we are. And Trent and Tony will probably grow up to be big jerks because their mom is as screwed up as the rest of us."

"I am not screwed up, Kaylin. I am a successful—"

"Holly was our one shot at being normal." Kaylin gave up appeasement and settled for full-blown fury. "But you ruined it for all of us, Rafe. She went running for her life because *you're so needy!*"

"Go to your room right now!" ordered Rafe.

Instead, Kaylin dashed out the back door straight to Holly's back door. Rafe was about to follow her—he got as far as their adjoined backyards—before he came to an abrupt halt.

Kaylin had truly outfoxed him. He couldn't go running after her, not when the kid had taken herself to Holly's place. Especially not after Holly had just accused him of being *needy!* She would probably assume that he'd put Kaylin up to it in a pathetic ploy to get inside. And since Kaylin wasn't exactly pleased with him at the moment, the brat would probably swear to it just to see Holly light into him again.

Rafe stood in the shadows and watched Holly open the door to Kaylin, saw her admit the girl inside.

"I hate my brother!" Kaylin announced dramatically as she flounced around Holly's kitchen. She ended up at the refrigerator and opened the door. "Can I have some fruit salad?"

"Help yourself." Holly handed her a bowl and a spoon. "Why do you hate your brother, Kaylin?" In the teenager's presence, it was easy to lapse into her usual role of helping adult.

Kaylin dug into the fruit salad. "He's so needy! I can't take it anymore."

Holly's face flushed scarlet. "You overheard our—argument."

"Yeah." Kaylin nodded vigorously. "I'm on your side, Holly. All men are pigs. Mom always said so."

"Kaylin, our mothers sometimes say things that they believe to be true but really aren't. All men are not pigs. Your brother certainly isn't. He cares about you very much. He wants to do what is best for you and tries very hard."

"Well, if he's so great, how come you couldn't stand to be with him tonight? I know you're sick of him, Holly. Are...are you sick of me and Camryn and Trent and Tony, too?"

Holly sank into a kitchen chair beside Kaylin. "Of course not, honey. I'm just...I'm in a bad mood tonight and I took it out on your brother." Which was the partial truth. No need to mention that Rafe had caused her bad mood in the first place.

"That used to happen to our mom. She'd have a bad day at work and then come home and yell at Camryn and me. I hate it when people are yelling. You were yelling at Rafe," Kaylin added accusingly.

"Yes, I was. I'm sorry you were upset, Kaylin, but it's normal for people to argue. It doesn't mean that...that..." Holly paused, swallowing hard. "That Rafe and I don't care about you and Camryn and the boys. We both do, very much."

"Do you still love Rafe?" Kaylin quizzed.

Holly looked away from the girl's probing gaze. "Kaylin, my feelings for you and your sister and the boys are separate from whatever goes on between Rafe and me. I want you to know that I'll always be your friend and—"

"Because Camryn says you don't love Rafe," Kaylin cut in.

"She says you're just using him for sex because he's convenient, being right next door and all. She says you'll blow him off whenever you meet somebody who'll give you what you really want."

"And what would that be?" Holly couldn't resist asking.

"Oh, you know. A cool life." Kaylin looked downcast. "Camryn says that life with Rafe is not cool for you. How could it be, when you have to put up with awful Flint and Eva who hate you? And Trent and Tony and Tracey, who will always need help? Not to mention me and Camryn who'll be grown up and gone soon but still..." She shrugged. "I thought you loved Rafe but Camryn says no. No way."

Holly would've laughed if she didn't feel like crying. Camryn, that young cynic, had gotten things precisely backward. Rafe was using her for sex because she was convenient, being right next door. And Kaylin was positively, absolutely on target. Holly loved Rafe but she wasn't about to tell his young half sister so. Not when he'd made it positively, absolutely clear that he was uninterested in marrying her.

"I think my life is quite cool right now, Kaylin." Holly forced a smile. "Remember when we talked about how important it is for people to make their own happiness and not to expect someone else to provide it?"

She would do well to remember her own homilies, Holly reminded herself.

"Yeah, I remember." Kaylin stood up. "Can I watch your TV?"

"What about your homework?"

"It's done. Please let me stay! I don't want to go home yet."

Holly felt caught in the middle, which she suspected was exactly what Kaylin intended. "You'll have to call your brother and ask him, Kaylin."

Holly left the kitchen to give the girl some privacy during the call. Kaylin joined her in the living room a minute or two later. "Rafe said he'll bow to your superior judgment," the girl said cheerfully. "And you say it's okay if I stay, right?"

Holly pretended she didn't get the dig inherent in Rafe's response. ''Fine. I'm glad you're here, Kaylin,'' she replied, knowing she would be quoted.

Hoping Rafe would get the dig inherent in her remark. That while she didn't want *his* company tonight, she did not mind Kaylin's.

Ten

A tense week followed.

If her life and her time weren't so inextricably woven into the lives of the four kids next door, Holly knew she would've avoided Rafe Paradise like the proverbial plague. She supposed he felt the same way about her because he made no effort to speak to her unless it had something to do with the children. Certainly, he didn't try to spend any time alone with her.

They were civil to each other while in the presence of the kids. Period. It was as if they were a divorced couple who tolerated each other strictly because of a joint custody arrangement.

Holly told herself it was best this way. Better to have found out his true feelings about her than to live in a delusional dreamworld where they were all one big happy family. She didn't mind her continuing involvement with Rafe's young half sisters and the Kriders; she'd come to genuinely care about them all. But she had no intention of being a convenient sexual outlet for the man next door. Who was completely uninterested in marrying her but had no qualms about using her body.

Rafe found it difficult to be around Holly. She was so competent and efficient and perfect with the kids, and so cold to him. But he didn't dare complain or even mention that he felt slighted, that he hated the change in their relationship because he didn't want to be perceived as *needy!*

When he wasn't missing her and the way things used to be between them, her accusation still infuriated him. He tried telling himself that he didn't need her, that he was an independent, high-functioning adult who didn't need anyone. Sometimes he almost convinced himself.

But while lying awake, tossing and turning in his lonely bed, Rafe tried to figure out what had gone so wrong. One night, around 3:00 a.m., he had an epiphany of such blinding clarity that he bolted upright in bed and gave up the pretense of trying to sleep.

The weather was growing cooler, and he pulled on a pair of gray sweats and an old U.S.D. sweatshirt to ward off the chill as he prowled restlessly through the house. The kids were all asleep in their rooms, and after growling a warning at him, Hot Dog settled down in his favorite spot at the top of the stairs and went back to sleep, too.

Rafe opened the front door and peered outside. All the way up and down the street, the houses were dark. Lights were on in only one place. In the other half of his duplex.

Acting on impulse, he walked over to Holly's front door and knocked. A few minutes later she opened the door to him.

She was wearing a fleecy pink bathrobe belted tightly around her. "Is something wrong?" She sounded genuinely concerned. "Are the kids—"

"They're okay." Rafe stared intently at her, until she began to squirm uncomfortably under the force of his gaze. *Good!* His eyes narrowed. "Can't sleep?" There was an unmistakable note of mockery in his tone.

"I was just reading," she replied defensively.

"Were you?" Rafe didn't wait to be invited inside.

He entered, forcing her to brush against him or else get out of his way. Holly opted for the latter, moving halfway across the room to avoid touching him. "Must be a pretty compelling read to keep you up till this hour, Holly."

Holly retreated to the sofa and picked up a book, which she held against her chest.

He walked toward her. "What are you reading?"

"A satire. It's hilarious. I've been laughing out loud."

Rafe tried to remember the last time he'd enjoyed a good laugh. That would be about a week ago, before Holly had turned into the Ice Queen. His sense of humor had been frozen since. "What's the title of this laugh riot?"

"The Rules," she replied, deadpan.

Rafe shrugged. "Never heard of it. Maybe you could lend it to me when you're finished?"

"Sure." Holly smiled tightly. *When hell freezes over.* "Why are you here, Rafe?"

"I remembered something you said about that dangerously suicidal patient of yours. The one with the abandonment complex that you were worried about leaving this weekend to go to your cousin's wedding."

"What made you think of that at three o'clock in the morning?"

"Nice try, Holly, but it's not going to work. You're not going to seize the offensive from me."

"I wouldn't dream of it. You're definitely more offensive than I could ever hope to be."

Rafe chose to ignore the insult. "That patient doesn't exist, Holly. That was the story you made up to use in case you decided not to go to the wedding," he declared triumphantly.

Holly's response was less than he wished for. "So?"

"So?" he echoed. His late-night epiphany suddenly seemed less clear. "That's what we were talking about the night we had that fight. And nothing has been the same since then, Holly. You know it hasn't." His eyebrows lifted and he frowned, as if daring her to contradict him.

Holly clutched the book more tightly against her, feeling the anger that had sustained her all week diffuse and weaken. This was not Slick Rafe, the smooth operator bent on using her; he was merely Rafe, confused and hopelessly dense. He actually didn't have a clue as to why things had abruptly gone sour between them.

After a whole week he'd managed to come up with the conversation that he thought had begun it all—not that he was even pretending to know why. Never mind that he'd forgotten the prelude to that conversation, the one that had *really* set their estrangement in motion. When he'd told her he didn't want to marry her. To give him his due, he believed that she didn't want to marry him, either.

Holly sighed. "Rafe, it's really late and we both have to get up early." She glanced at her small table clock. "In fact, we both have to get up about three hours from now."

"The hell with sleeping." Four giant steps put him directly in front of her. "I'm not tired." He pulled her into his arms and held her tightly against him, kissing her hair, her neck, her face. "I've missed you so much, Holly. I want you, I ne—" He broke off. No, he wasn't going *there*.

"Whatever I did, I'm sorry, Holly. I'm so sorry, baby."

She pulled back a little and gazed up at him. "Exactly what are you sorry for, Rafe?"

He swallowed. And decided to hell with his pride. "I did something that really upset you." It seemed an obvious guess.

"And you're so desperate for sex that you're willing to accept whatever blame I feel you should have?" Holly asked dryly. The book, sandwiched between them, pressed against her, digging into her ribs.

"I'm desperate for *you,* sweetheart. Sex is only part of it. Say you forgive me, Holly."

"I don't like the ways things have been with us, either, Rafe," she admitted. "But I'm not in the mood for a big makeup scene at this hour. I have a full patient schedule tomorrow and—"

His mouth covered hers, swallowing the rest of her words. He'd heard enough; she wasn't angry anymore. He didn't care to listen to whatever provisions she tacked on to the pardon she was granting him. He would deal with them later. Right now he wanted to taste her, to bury himself in her, to put an end to the intolerable distance between them.

Holly didn't even try to protest. It felt too good to be back in his arms. Her mouth opened under his the moment their lips met.

She decided that there was no reason why she and Rafe couldn't conduct an adult affair based on mutual pleasure and satisfaction.

Hearing Rafe declare that he was uninterested in marrying her had been an unpleasant shock, but like electroshock treatment itself, there were certain benefits to be derived. At least she was no longer a starry-eyed sap who believed that being in love was a necessary element for making love.

And reading *The Rules* tonight had delivered another jolt, reminding her of an important fact—that she was not obsessed with marriage. She never had been, something she'd managed to forget during the past intense and involved weeks with Rafe Paradise.

So what if he was uninterested in marrying her? She wasn't interested in having a husband and a wedding ring, anyway, Holly assured herself. Being Rafe's lover could be enough for her. She wanted him and he wanted her, so why shouldn't they have each other in bed? It could be that simple. Why should she overthink everything and make herself miserable?

Her Dr. Casale alter ego pointed out that she was overusing rationalization to justify her actions. Holly promptly shut her alter ego up. She emptied her mind of everything and kissed Rafe back, operating on sheer feelings.

His body was taut and hard against her, and she began to tremble, softening and molding herself to him. The book fell from her fingers to the floor, and they both ignored it as Rafe lifted her in his arms.

They were in her bedroom a few moments later, lying on the bed kissing and touching each other the way they'd been wanting to do every night during their long, lonely week apart. His sweats and her robe and silky pale pink nightgown were quickly discarded, and they both sighed as they lay skin-to-skin with nothing between them.

When Rafe slowed down to take his time with her, Holly urged him on. "I want you now," she breathed against his neck, clutching his firm buttocks with urgent fingers. "I want it fast and hard—and fast," she added again, just to make sure he understood.

She didn't want tenderness, she didn't want feelings, she

wanted sensation. Mindless, physical passion. Great sex. Who needed anything more?

Rafe delivered on all counts.

But afterward when they lay together, their bodies damp and replete and still joined, he stroked her hair and gazed into her eyes, looking...troubled?

"You seem different tonight," he murmured.

Holly closed her eyes. "Rafe, I'm too tired to talk. I need to sleep now."

"That's what I mean, you're different. You've never been too tired to talk."

"Well, I am now." She didn't open her eyes.

"I— You—" He paused, searching her face for a clue on how to proceed. But Holly appeared to be drifting off to sleep. "Was it good for you?" he heard himself ask. He cringed at the neediness in his voice.

So did Holly. Burgeoning emotions she could do without. "Rafe, you get two thumbs-up on your performance," she said lightly.

"It was more than just a performance, Holly," he admonished.

Holly's eyes snapped open. "Rafe, what do you want from me? I'm not angry, we went to bed, the sex was terrific. What else is there?"

"You didn't tell me you loved me," he blurted, suddenly struck by the omission. She always told him that she loved him, every time but this one. He realized how much he missed those softly whispered words. How much he needed to hear them.

He'd just had her body, yet he wanted her heart, mind and soul, too? The arrangement struck Holly as exceedingly one-sided, given his own limited involvement. He had made it clear that he did not consider their relationship to be headed toward permanence, toward marriage, and she was *fine* with that. However, accordingly, she had some limitations of her own to place.

Holly frowned. "Rafe, there are some—"

"Are you going to accuse me of being needy again?" Rafe cut in quickly. He didn't want to hear what she was going to say. Instinctively he knew he would hate it.

"Even after all the times you said it to me, I guess I've never told you that I love you, Holly."

He swallowed. He'd never said those words to any woman before. Though others might use them routinely, maybe even mean it at the time, he was not of that number. Saying *I love you* was the equivalent of making a major commitment. And because he always honored the commitments he made, he took great care before making one.

But he'd just said "I love you" to Holly. Rafe eyed her warily, wondering what to expect.

She didn't hop out of bed and suggest shopping for engagement rings. She didn't pick up the phone to book a place for their wedding reception.

She yawned. "It's cool. 'Night, Rafe." Closing her eyes again, she rolled onto her side.

"It's *cool?*" Rafe was thunderstruck. It sounded like something Camryn or Kaylin would say. It's cool. Everything was cool to them, except when it was uncool.

He suspected he was being uncool right now. He certainly felt that way. In fact, he felt burning hot with fury. But Holly appeared to have fallen into a sound sleep and though the temptation was mighty, he didn't awaken her and challenge her glib response.

Her earlier statement rang in his ears. *What do you want from me? I'm not angry, we went to bed, the sex was terrific. What else is there?*

He wished he had the answers to the questions she'd posed. For while he was glad—thrilled!—that she wasn't angry anymore, that they'd gone to bed and had terrific sex, he knew it wasn't enough. He wanted more from her.

His mind began to blur. The lateness of the hour caught up with him at last. He knew there was more but he couldn't figure out what it was and how to get it. Rafe turned on his side and pulled Holly closer to him, fitting her tightly against him, spoon-fashion.

She was sleeping deeply and didn't stir.

Holly kept insisting to Rafe that it wasn't necessary for him to accompany her to Heidi's wedding, right up until all six of them left for the airport. Each time she absolved him of going along with her, Rafe countered with an excuse as to why he had to go. Then it was her turn to refute the excuse.

When Rafe claimed that the plane tickets he'd bought for himself and the kids were nonrefundable, Holly called the airlines and was able to assure him that refunds were indeed available.

He said the kids were looking forward to the trip and he couldn't disappoint them by bowing out. Camryn sabotaged him by rolling her eyes and caustically proclaiming, "Oh sure, I'm just dying to go to *Michigan!* It's a dream come true for me."

But Kaylin said she didn't mind going, and Trent and Tony were wildly excited about taking their first flight. They were less enthused about the wedding itself, hoping to spend the time in the hotel instead.

Still, it was enough to allow Rafe to maintain his premise. He'd promised the kids a trip to Michigan, and he wasn't a man who reneged on his word. Especially not to children.

"Anyway, if I don't go with you, you'll be at the mercy of the chiropractor and your matchmaking relatives," Rafe reminded Holly, joking about the reason why she'd invited him in the first place.

Holly didn't seem to require the protection of his presence anymore. "I'll just tell the chiropractor that I have a lover in Sioux Falls, and I'll tell my family that my lover and I are perfectly content with our relationship exactly the way it is. I'll tell them once and for all to quit bugging me about getting married because I'm simply not interested."

Rafe wondered why her answer disturbed him so much. She'd only said what he himself had told Flint and Eva about their relationship. His twin and his younger sister asserted that Holly was laying a careful matrimonial trap for him culminating in the wedding trip to Michigan to meet her family, but Rafe was beginning to believe that devilish Camryn was closer to the mark.

"Holly doesn't want you to go to that wedding because she doesn't want to listen to her family blather on about how unsuitable you are for her. As if she doesn't already know that!" Camryn told Rafe after listening to Flint state the opposite.

"I am not unsuitable for Holly," Rafe stormed defensively, and Camryn shook her head, incredulous. "Dream on, Rafe! You're just a passing convenience for her. But why do you care, anyway? You're only using her, too."

"I am not using Holly!" he insisted to Camryn.

He wondered if Holly thought so and tried to assure her one night after a torrid lovemaking session that left him oddly unfulfilled. Not physically, of course. Sexually, they were ideally suited to each other. But something was missing, though he couldn't exactly pinpoint what.

He told Holly he wasn't using her, hoping for—something. She merely laughed and said, "Of course you're not." She did not care to discuss the matter further. Holly wasn't much for intimate talks these days.

He missed those talks they used to have after sex. Quiet, drowsy times when he would hold Holly in his arms and she would tell him what she thought, how she felt. He'd never said much but he had always liked listening to her. Now she wanted to go to sleep right after they climaxed. Shouldn't he be pleased that she was so undemanding? Shouldn't he be relieved that she did not require his attention and assurance?

Instead, he felt neither pleased nor relieved. It came as a distinct shock when he finally realized that he wanted Holly to make demands on him. Emotional demands. Any kind of demands.

But she didn't.

They arrived at the hotel where the wedding reception was to take place later the next evening, and where a contingent of out-of-town family and friends were already encamped for the round of prewedding festivities.

Holly had informed her relatives that she was bringing her "good friend" Rafe Paradise along, and that he would be accompanied by what she jokingly referred to as "his entourage," Camryn, Kaylin, Trent and Tony.

Aunt Honoria met Rafe and the kids and told Holly that she still hoped to introduce her to the chiropractor. "I think it's wonderful that you're helpful to Rafe and that you get along so well with those unfortunate kids, but he certainly isn't marriage material, not for you, Holly. A woman with a bunch of her own kids might consider him marriageable, but thank God you two are simply friends.''

Her mother and aunt Hedy were less convinced. For the first time in Holly's memory, they heralded the joys of the single life to her.

''Why tie yourself down?'' Aunt Hedy asked shortly after meeting Rafe and his entourage, raucous and noisy Trent and Tony, sullen and pouting Camryn and Kaylin. ''And taking on that crew would be like tying yourself to an anchor on a sinking ship. No matter what Mr. Paradise offers, no matter what he says, don't go beyond friendship with that man, Holly.''

''Having a family of your own is one thing, Holly,'' her mother cautioned. ''Of course you want your own baby. Perhaps more. But who wants four foster children and all the emotional baggage that comes with them? You practice psychiatry for a living, but enough is enough. Holly, steer clear!''

''They're not Rafe's foster children, Mom.'' Holly attempted to explain Rafe's relationships to the kids again.

Her mother wasn't interested in hearing the details. ''They live with him and he is legally responsible for them. That makes him their foster father. And I can just tell that he would like nothing better than to make you their foster mother. Who can blame him, of course. But, Holly, you're not *that* desperate to get married!''

Rafe was incensed. Holly's family, never subtle in their various campaigns, was equally open in their opposition to him. He sensed it, and then he actually heard with his own ears because the topic of Holly and himself and why she should run like hell from him was discussed constantly, openly, by the entire family. His *friendship* with Holly superceded every other subject, including tomorrow's wedding.

''I feel like a leper,'' Rafe complained to Camryn in their hotel suite late Friday night after enduring an evening of disconcerting stares, disapproving glances and overheard frantic warnings to Holly. ''Do you think Holly's family is prejudiced against Indians? Her sister looked like she expected me to don war paint and leap across the room to scalp her at any minute.''

''You *wish* it was simple prejudice,'' Camryn said archly. ''But it doesn't matter who or what you are. Holly's relatives think you're unfit because of the kids and me. They think we'll drag Holly down and ruin her life. Hey, maybe they're right.''

Rafe snorted his disgust. "I think that's Holly decision to make.''

"Yeah. Y'know, Holly fits in better with us. She is so much cooler than her family. I don't like any of them except Heidi, the bride. Heidi has potential. Too bad she's marrying that dork. Talk about lives being ruined!''

Rafe looked at Camryn in her short, shiny, purple dress, hideous '70s retro garb combined with equally alarming shoes, and felt a surge of loyalty to his often edgy, often conniving, frequently maddening kid sister. This time Camryn was absolutely right—Holly belonged with him and the kids, no matter what her relatives said.

He knew he had to see Holly and remind her of that critical fact. "If I call Holly and ask her to meet me in the hotel bar for drinks, will you stay here in the suite and keep an eye on the kids, Camryn?''

Trent and Tony were watching television in one bedroom and Kaylin was in the Jacuzzi in the luxurious bathroom. "Okay,'' agreed Camryn. "Can I have a friend over?''

"You don't have any friends in Michigan. Do you?''

"Heidi is a friend. I'm going to ask her if she wants to hang out for a while.''

Rafe frowned, considering. "I guess there's no harm in that. But I wouldn't count on her showing up, Camryn. Isn't she partying with the groom and their friends?''

Camryn was already on the phone when he left the room.

"Your family hates me.'' Rafe eyed his martini in the dimly lit, fern-infested bar not far from the bustling hotel lobby. He rarely drank but after the less-than-warm welcome from Holly's family, a stiff drink held definite appeal.

"They don't hate you personally.'' Holly slipped her hand under the table to rest it on his thigh. She was truly appalled by the clan's wholesale rejection of Rafe. "But they have been awful. I'm sorry, Rafe.''

"Don't apologize for them." His hand closed over hers. "After all, I've never apologized for the less-than-cordial way Flint and Eva treat you. Maybe I should have."

"Neither of us is responsible for the way our relatives behave, Rafe." Holly interlocked her fingers with his. "I'm glad you came with me."

"I am, too, baby."

"Even though it looks like we're in for a you-and-me-against-the-world kind of weekend?" Holly smiled at him, and the warmth and tenderness in her gaze took his breath away.

"As long as you're the one who's not against me, I don't care about the rest of the world, Holly."

"Me, either." She was touched by his declaration. And slightly drunk from the very strong martini. The combination caused her to abandon her usual reserve about public displays of affection. She inched her chair closer to Rafe's and leaned against him, kissing his hard, bronzed cheek.

He reacted at once, cupping her face with his hands to raise her lips to him. He slanted his mouth over hers and they shared a hot wild kiss that grew hotter and wilder.

"Holly!"

The sound of her name reverberated in Holly's head before it fully registered that someone was calling her. It wasn't Rafe, because he was kissing her.

But then he slowly lifted his lips from hers. Holly clung to him, reluctant to break the sweet intimacy enshrouding them.

"I thought you said that you two were just friends, Holly."

Holly heard the disembodied voice floating over her head. She and Rafe simultaneously turned to face two astonished brunettes, standing beside their table, staring down at them. Holly moaned and buried her face against Rafe's shoulder.

"We met earlier at the party following the rehearsal dinner," one of the brunettes said to Rafe. "I'm Holly's cousin Hillary and this is my sister Hayley."

"I remember meeting a brigade of women tonight, all with names beginning with H." Rafe wondered at the odd custom, and decided that when he and Holly had kids, none of them would have a name that began with the letter *H*.

"It looks to me that you two are more than friends," said one of the H cousins.

"We never saw Holly and her so-called *good friend* Devlin Brennan holding hands, let alone making out in a hotel bar," added the other cousin.

"We are more than friends," Rafe announced.

Holly's head popped up. "Yes," she agreed. "We're—"

"Going to be married," Rafe cut in before she could blurt that they were lovers. Although that was true, they were so much more. More than lovers, more than friends. Everything.

"I'm tired of pretending otherwise, Holly," he said, meeting her wide, brown eyes.

"Everybody here knows that this friendship bit is just a ruse. And if they haven't figured it out, they should've."

"Oh, my," said Hillary.

"I guessed it from the moment I saw you two together," Hayley said smugly. "Congratulations, both of you."

"You do realize that they're heading straight for a phone," Holly said to Rafe as her cousins beat a hasty retreat from the table. "Within ten minutes, my entire family will think that you and I are getting married."

"Good." He stood up and took both of her hands in his, pulling her to her feet.

"The kids have completely taken over the suite so we'll have to get another room to have any privacy tonight."

Holly swayed a little, and Rafe put his arm firmly around her waist and walked her out of the bar, toward the long desk in the lobby. "Dizzy?"

"A little." She blinked. Hillary and Hayley were each seated at a telephone in a phone bank that lined one end of the lobby. "I need some coffee. I'll need a clearer head to debunk the rumor about us that you just started."

"It's not a rumor, it's true. I'm going to marry you."

"Rafe, exactly how much did you have to drink tonight?"

"I had a taste of one martini, Holly. I'm not drunk." He stopped a few feet away from the registration desk and put his hands on her shoulders. "In fact, I've never seen things more clearly in my life. I love you, Holly, and you love me. Marry me, Holly."

"Last week you assured your brother that you weren't interested in marrying me," Holly blurted.

"Last week..." Rafe gave her a long, level look. She met and held his gaze. "Last week I was an idiot, Holly," he said softly, pulling her into his arms.

"I'm not about to argue with that." Her voice was muffled against his chest.

"Good, because I don't want to argue. I want to register for a room and make love to you. And propose to you."

Which he did, with passion and love and great finesse.

Holly accepted his proposal, emotional tears filling her eyes. She lay in his arms, feeling content and sated and truly loved. "I love you so much, Rafe. I never thought it was possible to love someone the way I love you. This past week—"

"Can we forget all about this past week?" Rafe interjected, his tone heartfelt. "I spent it in a state of abject misery, knowing that something was drastically wrong but not knowing what. You were so different. I missed you, even though you were right there with me, and I couldn't make any sense of it."

"You were so dense," Holly said sweetly.

"How long were you going to make me suffer?"

"I didn't have a particular plan, I wasn't following a guide book." Holly thought of *The Rules* and shivered. "I was just...protecting myself."

"You were an idiot, too," Rafe decided. "You forgot the shrink's first commandment—to communicate openly."

"I suppose I did," Holly murmured thoughtfully. She linked her arms around his neck and snuggled closer. "Never let me do that again, Rafe."

"I won't." He nibbled on her lips. "Never doubt how much I love you, Holly."

"Never," she promised.

He took a deep breath. "Holly, tomorrow your family is going to try to talk you out of marrying me. They'll tell you what a bad deal you're getting with me, and they are probably right."

"They couldn't be more wrong, Rafe. You're the man I've been waiting for my entire life."

Rafe sighed deeply, his face aglow with pleasure. "This is the way it should be, the way it wasn't last week. You, talking to me instead of rolling over and falling asleep immediately after making love."

"Me, telling you how wonderful you are." Holly smiled mischievously. "And you are wonderful, even if you are somewhat clueless at times. Last week I didn't fall asleep immediately afterward, Rafe. Not even once. I pretended to, but I was awake for a long, long time."

"I hope you were as miserable as I was." Rafe feigned indignation.

"At least as miserable," she assured him. "Maybe even more."

"You know exactly what to say to me." Rafe laughed softly and moved to lie on top of her.

Holly savored the feel of his warm weight upon her. She wrapped herself around him and welcomed him inside. Their eyes were locked as he surged into her, filling her. Joining the two of them into one, united in body and spirit.

Later, after more loving and more talking, they both fell into a deep, peaceful sleep.

The ring of the telephone awakened them the next morning. Jarred out of sleep, Rafe fumbled for the phone, his mind still clouded with dreams. He hadn't needed a dream catcher to trap any bad dreams last night. Having Holly in his arms in bed insured sweet dreams and a superior night's sleep.

"Are you going to sleep all morning?" Kaylin's teasing voice brought Rafe fully awake.

His eyes widened when he saw the digital clock on the nightstand. Ten o'clock! He couldn't remember the last time he'd slept so late. He couldn't remember the first time. *This* was the first time!

Beside him, Holly propped herself up on her elbow and smiled at him. Rafe forgot to feel guilty for sleeping so late. And then it struck him. "How did you know where I was, Kaylin?"

"Well, you weren't here," Kaylin said logically. "So I called the desk and asked for another room under your name. Congratulations, Rafe. I was worried you'd screw things up with Holly, but you didn't. You're going to get married! Tell Holly that Camryn and me are thrilled she's going to be a Paradise. I can't wait till Flint and Eva hear. They'll puke at the news!"

Rafe chose to overlook that last remark. "How do you know Holly is here?" he asked carefully. "And how do you—"

"Duh, Rafe! I know Holly's there with you and I know you two got engaged last night. We've only had about forty-five calls from her family this morning."

Rafe's hand tightened around the receiver. "Her family has been calling the room?"

Holly flopped back down and put the pillow over her face.

"Since this is your room, your first room, they thought you were here. They didn't think you might be hiding out somewhere else. Don't worry, I covered for you."

"What have you been telling them, Kaylin?" Rafe asked uneasily.

"Different things. That you and Holly are either in the Jacuzzi or in the shower or still in bed and that's why neither of you can come to the phone." Kaylin laughed. "They were shocked. *Shocked!* Want me to keep blowing them off? I thought I'd call to check."

"Well, since they're already shocked and probably consider me beyond redemption anyway, we may as well have breakfast before facing any of them. Could you stall them for another hour or so while we call room service, Kaylin?" Rafe lifted the pillow from Holly's head.

She was blushing. He traced the fine line of her jaw with his index finger. She caught his finger and kissed it.

"I can stall them all day, if you want. We already had room service bring us our breakfast," Kaylin said breezily. "Try the eggs Benedict, fresh fruit and assorted Danish. Oh, and the flavored coffee, too. The boys got hot chocolate with real whipped cream. It's all delicious."

"A breakfast like that probably cost about forty bucks apiece," Rafe muttered, but he was too happy to really mind the bill that the four had undoubtedly run up. And he was too glad for the chance to have some extra time with Holly to feel guilty about asking Kaylin to run interference with Holly's relatives.

He and Holly had a couple more hours alone together and he intended to make the most of them...

Holly decided to hide out at the hotel until shortly before the wedding, hoping to avoid for as long as possible the onslaught of questions, advice and warnings she knew would be forthcoming from various family members.

She and Rafe took Tony and Trent to the hotel game room where they played video games. She lay on a lounge chair with a magazine beside the indoor swimming pool while Rafe and the boys swam. Camryn and Kaylin declined to accompany them, preferring to stay in the suite.

About an hour before the wedding, she finally drove to her parents' home to get dressed for the ceremony. And to finally face her family's dire warnings about her upcoming marriage. Holly braced herself. Listening to them insist that she was better off single would be like stepping into "The Twilight Zone." Fortunately, her father would not offer an opinion, he never did. He and her uncles were quite content to let their wives deal with their daughters.

Holly knew Rafe would never accept such a nonrole in his own family. He was actively involved in his younger sisters' and Little Brothers' lives; he would do no less with his own sons and daughters. Who would be *her* children, too. Holly sighed as a wave of pure happiness swelled within her.

The Casale house was in chaos, with phones ringing, and the aunts and cousins frantically racing around. The men had retreated to the den to watch a Big Ten college football game on TV.

No one said a word to Holly about her engagement. That news had already been supplanted by today's current crisis.

"Heidi is missing!" shrieked Aunt Hedy. "Honoria thought she was sleeping late but when she finally went into her room around noon, Heidi wasn't there! Her bed hadn't been slept in last night!"

"Maybe she spent the night with her fiancé," Holly suggested. "Has anyone talked with him?"

"Of course we did!" snapped Heather, Heidi's sister. "He hasn't seen Heidi since they had a fight at the party after the rehearsal dinner last night. Apparently, Heidi didn't come home last night."

"Have you called her friends?" asked Holly.

"We contacted every name in her address book," said Holly's sister Hope, dabbing her eyes with a tissue. "Heidi isn't with any of them, although someone remembers seeing her driving alone in her car last night, after she'd left the party to go home."

"Have you notified the police?" Holly tried to stay calm, although she felt an ominous stirring in the pit of her stomach. She read the papers, she listened to the news. Terrible things could and did happen to young women, especially late at night.

"Honoria won't let us call the police." Holly's mother was distraught. "She is convinced that little Heidi is in one of her moods and will show up right before the wedding."

"'One of her moods'?" Holly stared at the group. "Heidi was never particularly moody."

"She's changed a lot since the engagement." Hayley finally spoke up. "She's become argumentative and negative."

"We chalked it up to premarital jitters," Hillary said morosely.

"Did Heidi ever express any doubts about getting married?" Holly quizzed.

The other women looked at each other. "We never took her seriously," Aunt Hedy said earnestly. "What young woman wouldn't want to have a big, beautiful wedding like the one we've been planning for Heidi?"

Holly remembered all the years she had resisted exactly that. It wasn't until she'd fallen in love with Rafe, a man she wanted to spend the rest of her life with, that she had finally considered marriage. And she had yet to think about what kind of a wedding they would have.

She had the feeling Heidi had reversed the sequence. The wedding occupied all her thoughts, plans, and dreams with marriage— and the prospect of spending the rest of her life with the man she was marrying—barely a blip on her psychic radar screen. Until last night?

"I hear there's a pretty good mall a few miles down the road," Camryn said, glancing through the room service menu. "With a multiplex theater and everything. Can I take the car and drive Kaylin and me down there."

Rafe, dressed in his suit for the wedding that was scheduled to begin in less than forty-five minutes, frowned his impatience. Camryn was still in jeans and a T-shirt. Kaylin had yet to return with the boys from the video game room. He knew they were still in their jeans and T-shirts, too.

"You can't drive the rental car, Camryn. And there is no time for a trip to the mall, anyway. Start getting dressed for the wedding. I'll find Kaylin and the boys and—"

"Oh, there's no rush. Hey, Rafe, I have a present for you." Camryn strolled across the room and rummaged through a drawer. She smiled triumphantly when she came up with a lacy blue garter, embroidered with white hearts. "This is for you. You can't catch it at the reception tonight, but Heidi wanted you to have it anyway. After all, you'll be getting married soon."

Rafe examined the garter. "I don't think it'll fit me, but thanks anyway."

"You're supposed to give it to Holly." Camryn grinned. "It'll fit her."

Rafe pictured it on his bride-to-be's shapely thigh. He imagined himself removing it and smiled wolfishly. "It'll fit her very nicely. Thanks, Camryn."

"It was Heidi's. Thank her the next time you see her." Camryn went back to the room service menu. "Can I order a snack?"

"No. You have to get ready for the—"

The phone rang and Rafe hurried to answer it.

"Rafe, Heidi is gone," cried Holly, her voice tremulous. "It's crazy over here, as you can imagine, and I just don't know what to—"

"Heidi is gone?" Rafe repeated. He glanced absently at the blue garter he was still holding in his other hand, then stared at

Camryn who had begun to paint her nails a startling shade of puce. "Holly says that Heidi is gone, Camryn."

"Yes." Camryn was nonchalant. "And she won't be back any-time soon."

Rafe felt as if he'd been kicked in the head. "Holly, you'd better come over here right now."

Camryn declined to talk about Heidi until Holly's arrival. "Why tell the whole story twice?"

Rafe didn't mind waiting. He didn't want to hear the whole story twice.

He pressed the lacy blue garter into Holly's hand when she arrived at the hotel suite. "This is Heidi's. Camryn passed it on to me. I'm fairly certain she knows where Heidi is and I have a sickening feeling she engineered the disappearance."

Camryn joined them, giving Holly her most angelic smile. "I'm so happy you and Rafe are getting married, Holly. That reverse psychology stuff really works, doesn't it?"

"Do you know where Heidi is, Camryn?" Holly asked anx-iously.

"On her way to Las Vegas." Camryn checked her watch. "Or maybe she's there by now. She took the bus, and I gave her the names and addresses of some really cool people I know out there. Most are about her age. I know she'll hit it off with them."

"Las Vegas?" Holly sat down hard on the edge of the bed.

"She left the garter for your wedding and this cheesy ring for the dope she dumped." Camryn produced Heidi's engagement ring. "We're supposed to give it back to him."

"Good Lord!" Rafe sat down beside Holly. "I thought this sort of thing only happened in bad TV movies."

"Why did Heidi go to Las Vegas without telling anyone, Cam-ryn?" Holly asked, trying to stay calm. It wasn't easy. She was already envisioning the brouhaha that would ensue when this news broke.

"Well, she told *me*." Camryn defended the runaway bride. "Heidi was desperate, Holly. She didn't want to marry that guy, but she didn't know how to get out of it. She said the wedding was like a train without brakes coming down the track at her. So

I said unless she wanted her life to be a train wreck, she should get out of the way fast.''

"Actually, that is solid, practical advice, Camryn," said Holly.

Camryn beamed. "I told her to buy a bus ticket and go to Las Vegas. It's a perfect place to start over. That's what my mom said when we moved there."

"This is bad, Holly." Rafe looked grim. "Your family didn't approve of me before. Wait till they hear my sister encouraged the bride to jilt the groom and hit the road for Vegas."

"I'm only sorry that poor little Heidi was unable to confide in anybody," Holly murmured. "She must have felt so desperate and alone. I wish she'd felt comfortable enough to tell me about her doubts."

"You've been busy, Holly." Camryn consoled her. "So I stood in for you. I'm thinking of maybe becoming a psychologist. I kind of have a knack for it."

Before Rafe could speak, Holly carried his hand to her mouth and pressed her lips against his palm. "My family is very lucky to have both you and Camryn, and that's what I intend to tell them, Rafe. After I call my aunt with the good news that little Heidi is safe and well in Las Vegas."

"We could round up the kids and go to that mall, Rafe," Camryn suggested hopefully. "Unless you want to be around when Holly gives the family the good news about Heidi's new life?"

"I'm not taking off and letting Holly face this mess by herself," Rafe said firmly. "We stick together."

Holly stroked his cheek. "When you're ready to get married, look for a man who is as gallant and brave and reliable as your big brother, Camryn. Don't settle for less, no matter how long you have to wait."

Camryn rolled her eyes. "I think I'll let you two alone to face the mess together. I'm going down to the game room and zap some aliens into the warp zone."

"Zap away." Rafe put his arm around Holly's shoulders and pulled her close. "We can handle anything as long as we're together, can't we, Holly?"

"Anything," Holly said, kissing him.

He held her hand as she picked up the phone to share the good news.

* * * * * *

Don't miss Barbara Boswell's next story,
a brand-new novella featured in
A FORTUNE'S CHILDREN CHRISTMAS,
coming from Silhouette Books this December!

SILHOUETTE®

Desire®

For nearly ten years Silhouette Desire has been giving readers the ultimate in sexy, irresistible heroes. And you'll find those same gorgeous men tempting you to turn every page in the upcoming sensual, emotional **Man of the Month** love stories, written by your favorite authors.

MAN
of the
Month

Available at your favorite retail outlet.

Take 2 bestselling love stories FREE

Plus get a FREE surprise gift!

Special Limited-Time Offer

Mail to Silhouette Reader Service™

3010 Walden Avenue
P.O. Box 1867
Buffalo, N.Y. 14240-1867

YES! Please send me 2 free Silhouette Desire® novels and my free surprise gift. Then send me 6 brand-new novels every month, which I will receive months before they appear in bookstores. Bill me at the low price of $3.12 each plus 25¢ delivery and applicable sales tax, if any.* That's the complete price, and a saving of over 10% off the cover prices—quite a bargain! I understand that accepting the books and gift places me under no obligation ever to buy any books. I can always return a shipment and cancel at any time. Even if I never buy another book from Silhouette, the 2 free books and the surprise gift are mine to keep forever.

225 SEN CH7U

Name	(PLEASE PRINT)	
Address	Apt. No.	
City	State	Zip

This offer is limited to one order per household and not valid to present Silhouette Desire® subscribers. *Terms and prices are subject to change without notice.
Sales tax applicable in N.Y.

UDES-98   ©1990 Harlequin Enterprises Limited

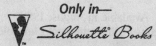

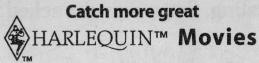

MARILYN PAPPANO

Concludes the twelve-book series—36 Hours—in June 1998 with the final installment

YOU MUST REMEMBER THIS

Who was "Martin Smith"? The sexy stranger had swept into town in the midst of catastrophe, with no name and no clue to his past. Shy, innocent Julie Crandall found herself fascinated—and willing to risk everything to be by his side. But as the shocking truth regarding his identity began to emerge, Julie couldn't help but wonder if the *real* man would prove simply too hot to handle.

For Martin and Julie and *all* the residents of Grand Springs, Colorado, the storm-induced blackout had been just the beginning of 36 Hours that changed *everything*—and guaranteed a lifetime forecast of happiness for twelve very special couples.

Available at your favorite retail outlet.

Silhouette ®

The World's Most Eligible Bachelors are about
to be named! And Silhouette Books brings
them to you in an all-new, original series....

World's Most
Eligible Bachelors

Twelve of the sexiest, most sought-after men share
every intimate detail of their lives in twelve never-
before-published novels by the genre's top authors.

Don't miss these unforgettable stories by:

Dixie Browning

MARIE FERRARELLA

Jackie Merritt

Tracy Sinclair

BJ James

RACHEL LEE

Suzanne Carey

Gina Wilkins

VICTORIA PADE

MAGGIE SHAYNE

Anne McAllister

Susan Mallery

Look for one new book each month in the
World's Most Eligible Bachelors series beginning
September 1998 from Silhouette Books.

Silhouette®

Available at your favorite retail outlet.